# The Meeting Place

## RUTH ROSENHEK

FREEFALL

First published in 2025 by FreeFall Publications, Australia
Copyright © 2025 Ruth Rosenhek

Cover design by Johanna Evans
Cover artwork by Ruth Rosenhek and Johanna Evans

ISBN (pbk) 978-1-7638176-5-4
ISBN (Kindle) 978-1-7638176-2-3

## Acknowledgement of Country

The writer and the setting of this book take place on the unceded lands of the Widjabl Wiabul and Githabul peoples of the Bundjalung Nation. I pay deep respect to the First Nations peoples who have lived here in relationship with and custodianship of this land for tens of thousands of years. I acknowledge their continuing connection to Country and recognise that sites in this fictional story are ones that carry deep spiritual and cultural significance for First Nations people and are places of real-life dispossession and trauma. In another thousand years, I pray this period of colonisation, oppression and exploitation of both people and Country will be a mere blip in a much longer history of respect, relatedness and reciprocity.

# Prologue

## March 2022

## Sara

The bridge is destroyed just seconds after I make it to the other side. With a deafening crash, it breaks loose, upturns and floats on its side down the creek. I lurch forwards in my car and accelerate up the hill. My heart pounds. Seconds before, I made the decision to cross the bridge despite the fast-rising foot high water. Flash flooding. That could have been me floating down the river.

It had been a harrowing drive home from the coast. The road has collapsed in some places with unannounced pits the size of a caravan. Elsewhere landslips have left boulders scattered haphazardly like pebbles strewn across the winding road west of Uki.

Just before telephone reception was lost, I received a text from Lissy saying "Water up to my waist. Me and the kids heading up to the roof, hopefully someone will come rescue us!" "See you once the waters subside, you'll be okay xx" I wrote back, knowing how Lismore becomes one big sea of currents and floating debris in events such as this.

I hate to say I told you so but this is all to be expected. We have truly messed things up now. Drought and bushfires that give way to cyclones and floods. And don't forget to throw in a pandemic or two along the way. I steady myself as I drive the rest of the way back to the community where I live. There is no way out other than the bridge and we will be hunkering down together, just as we did during the pandemic. Until a new bridge is built. I am looking forward to my nightly red wine and those chocolates I was going to give to Sandy for Valentines Day, before we broke up. Fortunately, my car is full of groceries. We'll be right, mate. I chuckle to myself softly. I am not afraid to have a laugh even when all hell breaks loose.

# Part 1 Round-up Day

## June 2028

# 1    Gale

Gale's office at Summerland Bank was located on the third floor of Molesworth Street, bordering the Wilsons River in the Lismore CBD. Her office had been one of the more fortunate ones, staying dry as the 2022 floodwaters receded and barely missing a beat. It was six years later now and Gale popped the last of a cheese and lettuce on multigrain into her mouth. Then, as was her habit, she walked past the elevator and bounded down the steps to the street below. She commended herself for slipping in a lunch break despite the extremely busy day she was having at the bank, where she managed an overworked IT department.

Gale stepped out of the air conditioning into a blast of heat. She wore flat, practical shoes, tailored grey slacks and a comfortable blue cotton business shirt. She had just enough time for a quick power walk under the shade of the towering bamboo stands that lined the banks of the river, sometimes a threatening force but now a deflated-looking muddy swamp. The exercise would keep her mind focused through the rest of the afternoon as she worked her way through the tedium of quarterly reports. The humidity hit her like a steaming laundromat. Gale ignored it and moved her 165-centimetre slender frame at a quick pace, weaving her way through the lunch crowd along the footpath.

An overhead plane reminded her of the drop-off just that morning at the Ballina airport. Emma, thirteen years of age and Gale's only child, had headed off to Western Australia, where her father, Jeff, lived. While Gale thought of Jeff as somewhat dull – in fact, this spelled the demise of their uneventful marriage several years ago – he was certainly steady and could be counted on to keep Emmy safe. They had started planning this journey after the floods, when Em's asthma started playing up at the tail end of the triple La Niña. When the rains gave way to prolonged heat and drought, Em's health had improved slightly, yet her lungs had continued to strain and their GP was concerned it could put Emma at higher risk of the latest strain of H7 avian flu that had broken out in New South Wales. All children over the age of three were mandated into lockdown conditions in their homes, while Western Australia had been more fortunate, with few viral outbreaks, and the cooler air at this time of year would be just what Emma's lungs needed. In a bold move, WA Governor Albright had shut the state's borders to the rest of the country; however, family members were still permitted to enter and domestic travel was open as long as travellers tested negative forty-eight hours before departure and home-quarantined on arrival. Gale would miss Emmy madly, their evenings around the television, morning walks, even the bickering they often fell into. She wanted Emmy to stay healthy but still she worried whether this was the right decision. Now it would be just Gale and Toby, her Jack Russell, at the ochre brick house she loved, an affordable home she had bought years ago on the edge of East Ballina, just a half hour from where she worked in Lismore.

A siren blared down the street bursting through Gale's thought bubble. A large black truck came barrelling along, followed by several windowless buses, also charcoal black.

The truck neared and Gale read the words "NSW Public Order Department" printed in bold white letters on the dark panels of the large cargo area. A black-and-white chequered pattern stretched the length of the truck's tray. Some sort of state government operation, she mused.

Gale and everyone around her stopped in their tracks. The back doors of the truck's cargo bay opened with a clashing of metal on metal and dozens of bodies descended, carrying the weight of head-to-toe riot gear: black padding strapped back-to-front across their midriffs, tasers and pistols in belt pockets slung around hips, helmets with dark wraparound goggles and a tight black stretchy material hugging their faces, extending below their eyes and down to their necks.

"This is the state police," announced the megaphones pitched in different directions on the truck's roof.

"This area is being evacuated. This is a public health emergency. Please board the nearest bus. Do not run."

There is no way I am going on that bus, thought Gale, as she picked up her pace to turn down the alleyway next to the Bank Cafe.

"Not so fast, young lady." A hand grabbed her elbow. Gale turned her head towards the hulking figure and attempted to pull her arm back.

"Don't touch me," she said angrily. Gale hated being called "lady" in any circumstances, let alone these. "You have no right to do this!" she proclaimed.

"Law Enforcement Power and Responsibilities Act 2028," the officer informed her.

Coincidentally, Gale's nephew had recently been remanded under this Act after his ex-girlfriend accused him of pushing her to the ground.

"That's for drink driving and DV," Gale insisted using her most authoritative voice.

"That's right, as well as evacuations under emergency declarations of health and safety, amended in parliament last week. Now come with me," he said curtly leaving no room for argument.

The officer exerted a piercing pressure on Gale's bicep and pulled her towards the bus, giving Gale no choice but to go along. Around her people were being corralled just as she was. Across the road there was shouting and pushing that was quelled within moments by a posse of authorities. Gale's eyes narrowed as she scanned for an opportunity to break free. She could feel the sweat under her arms against the cotton fibre running down her chest underneath the singlet she wore beneath her meticulously pressed shirt. Her thoughts spun wildly. It was terrifying to be rounded up like this but, more immediately, Gale was panicking at the thought of being in a dark, enclosed and overcrowded bus. That many people made her heart pound in her ears.

"No, no, I can't go in there!" she said. "I can't."

"In you go," the officer said as he pushed her up the steps.

Inside, the bus looked like any other bus except for the lack of windows, which made it a metal tank. Gale quickly grabbed a seat at the front, close to the door. She took her mobile out of her handbag to ring Mike back at the office.

No reception. Both phone and internet service were out of operation, the letters SOS displaying in the top right-hand corner of the screen. She tried 000 to no avail.

"Let me go!" a tall, older woman dressed in a light paisley frock and sunhat screamed at the guards as she was roughly pushed through the door before it swung shut. "My dog is still outside! You can't do this." She was banging on the closed door now. "Let me out!"

"Come on people, we need to leave. Now!" someone else chimed in, her voice cutting through the darkness.

"Where are they taking us?" shouted another woman as she jumped to her feet.

Looking around, Gale could see they were all women on this bus. She watched as bodies began pushing and shoving in the corridor, trying to get back to the door. Gale's mind clicked away. This couldn't be for their safety, there had been no advance notice given. She rose to her feet as well, just as a digitised voice came through the speaker inside the bus.

"Ladies and gentlemen, please take a seat. This bus is now departing." It was a melodious female intoned voice, the kind encountered in transport vehicles as well as elevators and cyber technology. Gale could hear and feel the bus begin to move but she was unable to see the world outside. With no driver, the front windscreen of the auto-drive bus was completely darkened. Gale started counting her inhalations to fight off a panic attack. The sound of sobs and angry voices caused her breath to quicken further as she tried to calm herself by picturing the vehicle's movements in her mind.

Straight for a couple of blocks, then left, right, left and right again.

It was only a matter of minutes, perhaps five at most, before they arrived at their destination. They must be at the showground, where the state government had reclaimed the land in 2027 to build an airtight quarantine facility. She had seen the high barbed-wire fence that had been erected and the building was a good ten storeys high. At least they were still in town, maybe it was just a temporary evacuation due to a new strain of virus or some other threat to public health. Gale shuffled through different scenarios in her mind, trying to make sense of what was happening. The worst of these painted a picture that was more like a scene from the Holocaust, mustard gas being released in the vehicle before they even had a chance to disembark. But the bus came to a stop and Gale was relieved to hear the voice instruct them to disembark.

As Gale and the others left the bus, they were greeted by a banner hung between two poles that announced, "NSW Department of Public Health Quarantine Facility". Gale had read about these new tech-sophisticated (tech-soph) facilities; they were everywhere in Australia, policed by robo-guards, as they were commonly known, and digitised through and through with voice-activated technology.

Gale and the others' voices rang out in random rapid fire as they descended from the bus onto a concrete pad that was enclosed by a fence covered in dark mesh.

"Let's stick together."

"We need to figure a way out."

"I need to get home to my children."

"How can they do this!"

Other than a large green plastic bin, nothing was visible except the hazy light-blue sky above and six guards standing around the periphery of the enclosed area. The guards, all female, wore casual uniforms of button-down khaki shirts, grey pants and solid work boots. Around their waists were belts that boasted a pistol on each hip.

"Please put all belongings in the bin before you enter the building," a voice boomed from a speaker mounted on a sign similarly instructing passengers. They headed through a door equipped with a security screening facility like those used in airports. "That includes your phones, watches, jewellery … just your body and your clothing as you enter."

"I'm not taking off my wedding ring!" protested a thin young woman in high heels and a tight-fitting red dress as her turn came to go through the security screening. Two guards swiftly surrounded her, forced the ring off and tossed it to the bin, then escorted her to the security screen.

The same plight befell another who refused to leave her phone behind. "I need my phone. My whole life is in there," she sobbed, tears streaming down her cheeks.

Gale and the other fifty or so women along with a few very young children were herded into a long room lined with white folding chairs spaced 2 metres apart, typical of pandemic social distancing. Gale fanned her shirt away from her body trying to cool herself down in the hot air being pushed around by two large fans in opposite corners, nowhere near enough to provide any relief.

"Attention. Please take a seat in the waiting area," a voice calmly spoke through inconspicuous speakers built into the corners of the room. "This facility is operated by robo-guards that are centrally controlled from Sydney. Please sit quietly – do not speak to anyone. Do not deviate from these instructions."

Gale nabbed a chair that was near the passageway in case there was an opportunity for a quick escape. Her eyes quickly scanned the perimeter and the guards positioned every 5 metres. She looked around at who was here with her – women of all ages in work clothes and everyday town errand clothing, a couple of very young toddlers and one infant. Older children would still be at home under isolation rules. There was mayhem in the room as many of the women cried for help while others spoke in urgent tones to each other. Gale's heart pounded in response and she tapped her thumbs against her index fingers as she worked to slow her exhalations.

After the last of the women had entered the room, the entry door swung shut with a clang. A wiry brunette in her twenties shrieked and pushed the woman next to her out of the way as she ran to the door and tugged on it frantically, desperate to pull it open. One of the guards swiftly moved towards her, grabbed her by the arm, lifting her off her feet, and plopped her down into one of the metal chairs. That guard is certainly not human, Gale thought. The room went into a hush. The women dared not look into each other's eyes where they could see their own terror reflected like daggers.

"Here we go again!" an Aboriginal woman in her later years yelled out.

"We gotta get out of here!" another voice shouted. "We outnumber them! We can rush back down the passageway. Now's our chance!"

"That door is locked! We can't get out!" the brunette exclaimed. A handful of women sprang out of their chairs and huddled together, everybody talking at once.

Gale looked around the room and spotted Shazz, the financial officer at Community Services. They caught each other's eye, resting there for a moment, fear silently communicated, then turned away.

"ORDER!" said the voice. "Everybody remain calm and return to your seats. I repeat, please remain calm and be seated now."

A mob of six or seven women rushed past Gale towards another door at the far side of the room. A half dozen guards quickly removed their tasers and aimed at the women, intercepting their movement. A zapping sound echoed off the brick walls and a young person in shorts crumpled to the floor.

"Hey, you can't do that." A woman who could have been the young one's mother confronted the guards who surrounded them.

"Go back to your seats now," one of the guards said.

"We have rights!" she demanded angrily. "Let us out of here!"

Gale watched as the woman was tasered on the spot and left in a pile on the floor. The remaining women returned to their seats, an edgy silence in the room.

One by one the women were asked to come forward and were escorted by a guard through the far door. Gale would be one of the last to leave as she sat on the other side of the room by the entry. No information was provided as to their plight, where they were going, what they were doing here. She turned her head slowly towards the guard standing a metre away from her at the back left-hand side of the room.

"Excuse me." She did her best to use a respectful and calm voice. "Could you tell me where we are being taken to?"

"Medical check," the guard replied.

"Medical check?"

"Yes."

"And then what will happen?"

"Wait your turn," the guard said officiously, terminating the conversation.

When Gale's turn arrived, only a few others remained in the room, sitting further along the back row. She got up tentatively and followed the official through the door, down another corridor and into a room that resembled a standard GP medical room with a hazardous-waste disposal bin, antibacterial units on the wall, sink, examination table, a couple of chairs and the pervasive smell of disinfectant.

"Have you ever been sick with H9?" asked a woman in a white medical coat.

"No," Gale uttered and. before she could protest, the medic briskly prepped Gale's arm and inserted a needle.

"A blood test to check for viral markers," she said.

Gale regained consciousness as her blood was being drawn into a series of test tubes. She felt her pulse quicken.

She tried to speak out but was unable and when she tried to get up, she could not move. She was paralysed. Her eyes darted rapidly around the room seeking information that would help her to understand what was happening. The medic continued to hunch over her and draw blood into a test tube that was neatly placed along with five others in a carrier that stood on a table with wheels. Gale flicked her eyes over to her other arm just in time to see a male medic completing a stitch in her wrist and Gale realised she had been implanted with a microchip. Wrist-tech was now widespread across Australia but still not mandated, and Gale had resisted using it for the past year. Her friends in IT teased her for being old fashioned but Gale stuck to her guns. She had strong reservations about having a chip implanted into her body, becoming even more easily tracked and observed by the system.

Being watched had snuck up in their lives. First, at schools, then CCTV cameras everywhere, as well as tracking through their phones and devices. To keep them safe, the authorities said. All computer screens became cameras that allowed the government to watch people in their homes, in the city and even in the desert, the remote regions. When the wrist microchip was introduced – you waved it over the "Quick Response", or QR, reader – some embraced this new technology without a qualm while others openly resisted. Not yet mandatory but highly "encouraged" as more and more places were only accessible with the chip. Easy and free access for one and all. Young people seemed to go right along with the whole thing but Gale had been reluctant, and her friends, Sara and Lis, even more so. Resisters, they were dubbed by the media. If you resisted, then no daycare for your children, no single parent benefit and eventually there would be no access to most public venues, let alone public transport. Even though Gale had worked in IT her whole life, she did not want bits and bytes to inhabit her body. This crossed a line she was not willing to cross. Until now. Gale tried to speak but instead a series of disjointed sounds tumbled sideways from her mouth.

"Waabanaoya bala."

"Don't try to speak," the woman said. "We are taking blood for the emergency blood bank. You have been tested for several coronavirus strains and a microchip with additional features has been implanted into your wrist."

"Icaaaaamooove," Gale said.

"Yes, that's normal. You were given a paralytic serum to make things easier. It's already begun to wear off and you'll be as good as new shortly. Then you'll be taken to your room."

"This facility is managed using wrist-tech," said the man. "If anyone does not follow instructions, the wrist-tech will render them temporarily immobilised, much like a nerve block might do if you have surgery. Much like you are experiencing right now."

About five minutes passed and Gale felt first her fingers and hands, then her arms and legs, regaining muscle control slowly to a background of pounding in her head. The door to the room opened and a woman with short brown hair, dressed in a button-down khaki shirt and well-pressed black pants, stood like a steel pole in the doorway.

"Follow me," she said.

"Where are you taking me?" Gale was relieved to be able to speak and move once again. "This is against the law."

"You are being quarantined; this is a public health emergency. Please do not speak any further," she commanded. "Now come with me."

Gale did not move. Thoughts madly raced through her mind searching for a way out of this situation. She did not see any escape routes and she was certain that she did not want to test out the paralysis that had been threatened.

"Now," the woman repeated with a little more emphasis and, while she was not visibly armed, she strode into the room swiftly and reached out to Gale's forearm to get her moving. Her grip was forceful, almost pulling Gale off her feet and down the corridor into another large room where a dozen or so women were at various stages of undressing, showering and being clothed. The guard instructed Gale to remove her clothing, drop it in the large bin, rinse off under one of the shower heads built into the wall on the other side of the room, and then proceed to the table piled high with clothing, where she was to find her size and get dressed.

Gale hesitated to take off her clothing. She was not one to remove her clothes in public places like the swimming pool or the gym, and this felt callous and crude. It stank of the dehumanising processes that occurred at Australian offshore detention centres.

"We have to get out of here!" cried a young Asian woman in blue jeans and a green singlet. "This could be our last chance. I have to get back to my children!"

All eyes in the room turned towards the woman. None of the half dozen guards made a move as the woman quickly pivoted to race towards the door and promptly dropped to the ground moaning.

Everybody moved quicker now. Gale removed her clothing and then stood briefly under tepid astringent water that sprayed out weakly from the showerhead.

"Attention. Be ready to leave this room in three minutes," the voice from the overhead speaker said.

Gale and several other women, still dripping with water, walked quickly over to the tables neatly stacked with clothing: grey trackies and hoodies, off-white T-shirts, black socks and laceless slip-on sneakers. Gale hurriedly selected clothing from the size-12 pile only to discover she had misjudged. The trackies would not stay up. For a moment panic set in as she looked for another pair, but there were none left.

"You have one minute left to complete dressing."

She scanned the group standing around the table and spotted a woman slightly larger than herself who was also looking around frantically. This woman clearly had pants that were too small for her. Quickly and without a word the two women exchanged the pants and finished dressing.

A buzzer sounded.

"You will now be accompanied to your accommodation."

The guards surrounded the women and in groups of ten instructed them to parade single file through a doorway and up a staircase. Gale's group was ushered to the eighth floor where they exited the stairwell to a corridor that had five rooms running off it, then around a bend to five more rooms. Ten to a floor. One by one they were accompanied by the guards to stand next to a metal door and enter their room.

"Please scan your wrist-tech to open your door."

Gale held her wrist up to the QR reader. A room of my own, she thought wryly as the door swung open automatically. A stuffy, hot concrete cell. Gale's breath quickened at the compact size of the room. Everything was crammed in: bed, tray-size table protruding from the wall, metal chair. Barely enough room to walk back and forth. She closed her eyes for a moment as she felt her body tilting to the side, off balance.

Gale reassured herself that this would only be a temporary measure; it was a quarantine facility. Perhaps they were genuinely being brought here while a new strain of virus hit the Northern Rivers. But why wouldn't the usual isolation orders be put into place, why would everybody be removed from town and why were they subjected to a cruel and militarised treatment with no information? The door swung closed. She was exhausted and alone in the dark cubicle. Gale sat down on the cold metal bed in the corner. Her mind looped busily for hours until eventually she passed into unconsciousness.

She woke up a few hours later. For a split second, she was in her bedroom at home but then the hardness of the thin mattress startled her back into the cold reality. She sprang up. Alert. Eyes open. Afraid to look. Forcing herself to look. A searing pain stabbed her temples as she rubbed her forehead. Her wrist throbbed uncomfortably. She steadied herself as her eyes bounced off the four concrete walls and floor. She cast her mind back, then reeled the line in as she reviewed the events of the past day. The bus, those who protested being tasered to the ground, the so-called advanced wrist-tech being implanted against her will, the humiliation of the communal shower and now this grey concrete cell. Her heart raced, the rapid pulsing visible in the rise and fall of her chest, like an accelerating drum roll. It had been over a year since she had experienced a panic attack. She closed her eyes, leaned forward with hands on knees and focused on slowing her breath while she pushed the balls of her feet onto the floor. She tried to conjure an image of Toby lying comfortably at her feet. After several elongated breaths, Gale opened her eyes tentatively to look around the cubicle. On the wall to one side of the bed was what appeared to be a squat toilet, no seat. Metal like almost everything else in the room. She stepped over to examine it further. A chemical smell wafted up; it was a non-flush drop toilet. She urinated down the hole and the liquid fell without a sound to the cistern below. She pictured herself dropping down through the opening; it would definitely be a tight fit. Too tight. Hands above head, down a concrete tunnel into what she imagined might be a slurry of shit and piss, and chemicals. Disgusting. Gale winced, lips pulled outwards.

Next to the toilet mounted on the wall was a push button with a bare-bones faucet just below aimed at a grate, bolted to the floor. She pushed the button tentatively and a few drops of water fell from the spout. Her own water dispenser, how thoughtful. Not exactly a waterfall but enough to wash her face and hands and to have a small drink. She wrinkled her nose in distaste at the metallic tasting water. The grim truth of her situation dropped like a bomb that closed the walls in on her as her stomach lurched, unable to control the horrific slideshow that her mind played scene by scene: pictures of calves squashed into trucks being corralled to a slaughterhouse, then men and women perched on the edge of vast pits awaiting execution until falling forward and landing criss-crossed over each other like icing on a hot cross bun. She squeezed her eyelids shut to stop the images.

"Agh!" she gave her head a vigorous shake.

The sound echoed off the walls of the chamber and caught in her throat. Eyes teared up. Breath wheezed. Uneven. Her head throbbed as if large pliers were being wrapped around her temples. She raised her shoulders up, neck a tight coil, teeth clamped together until finally a sob escaped. Then another sob. She tucked into a tight ball on the mattress. This was all she had left. A mattress that was fast becoming familiar. She tried to zoom in on a picture of her garden, her house, a place of safety – without success. She gave a start as she heard her voice crying out, her body tilted back and forth, rocking, as it had in her youth. No way out. Gradually, her sobs subsided to whimpers that cradled her back to sleep.

# 2    Lis

It started like any other day. Lis woke up to the sun peeking
through a gap in the yellow daisy curtains. Lately the rise
and set of the sun were magnificent. She knew the colourful
palette was a sign of all the smoke and dust storms passing
through the area yet, nonetheless, she was fully enraptured
by the amber, burnt orange and sienna blend. *Lost in Colour.*
That had been the name of her last exhibition at the Lismore
Regional Gallery. Her ability to get lost in art had been an
uncanny refuge from the state of the planet, like none other.
"Magnificent exuberance of colour," wrote the *Herald*'s art
critic. "It is as if Lis Waterman lives on a different planet. Her
world is unencumbered. Joyous." And it was true. Although,
it's not like I'm oblivious, she thought, I just don't see the
need to dwell on these things. Especially those things I can't
do anything about.

Lis rolled out of her comfy queen-size bed, pulled a
loose purple smock over her head and drew the strings of the
baggy, blue-striped Thai pants around her waist. She never
did lose the weight she put on after her firstborn, Sal, and then
David had arrived but she wasn't going to worry about that
now. Afterall, if she had been born in another era, she would
be a Rubens woman, plump in size and full of sensual appeal.
At the last minute, she decided to drape a multicoloured
Andean-looking cotton shawl over her shoulders to add a bit
more flair and to keep her neck warm in case it was cold in
the shop; she wasn't sure if the supermarket still offered air
conditioning to counteract the glaring heat. Lis was looking

forward to her outing as she headed down to the kitchen to make her morning coffee. Her stash of coffee beans was getting low and they were no longer available even in the specialty shops so she had cut back to a mere half shot each morning combined with powdered malt, not as tasty as the real thing but it did the job.

As usual, David was not yet up and about. All schools had been suspended across the nation since the H9 avian flu mutation started broadly infecting children between the ages of three and fifteen. Children from developed nations such as Australia, Canada, the US and across Europe were severely impacted. Most were getting through the virus itself but many were left with the dreaded Kawasaki disease and Reye's syndrome. Strangely, Reye's, known to develop when aspirin was used during viral illnesses, was now appearing despite the absence of aspirin, and lots of children were hospitalised and even dying of complications. Another thing Lis did not care to dwell on.

David and his friends were under stay-at-home orders and remained close to home, while Lis and other mothers ventured out donning face masks, toddlers in tow, for groceries and other home necessities. Today was her designated day to go shopping. Every household had been assigned one day a week to go food shopping, get goods from the chemist and any other essential items. The rest of the week she stayed at home with David, puttering around in the yard, cleaning and working on art projects in the house as usual, keeping David occupied with home schooling and other activities such as repairs and maintenance of their two-storey home. In the afternoons, neighbours congregated on the streets in what looked like a human chequerboard, carefully spaced 2 metres apart.

The grass was mostly dead around the houses. Water was restricted to 25 litres per day per person in each household. This was so very little that Lis and her children washed with a cloth and bowl and the rest was used for drinking, cooking and cleaning dishes. The rainwater tank had a meagre few hundred litres left that they occasionally drew off to wash some of their clothing in buckets. Oh, how she missed her long, hot showers.

About a year ago, a mouse and rat plague had scourged the state. Farmers' crops were annihilated. Children were waking up with mice in their beds, crawling over their faces. Like a scene out of a Stephen King novel. Electricity outages were frequent as rodents ate through wires and house fires started up, with some being burned to the ground, across central-west New South Wales and along the coast. Narrabri, Coonabarabran, Dubbo through to Forster, Nerang, Maitland and Newcastle. Sydney would be hit next. Lis was astounded that rats and drought could cause so much trouble. It was strangely poetic, she mused. Plague species, both rodents and humans. She had started working on a series of multimedia artworks featuring people with pointy-nosed rodent faces sitting around their swimming pools drinking martinis and G&Ts. A surreal project that brought a wry smile to her face when she conjured it up.

But it didn't bring a smile to the affected people who pleaded with the government to do something. Well, the government did something all right. The government assured its citizens that the previously outlawed broma-something-or-other, a rodenticide, would be just what was needed and ordered citizens to stock up on food supplies as they would need to stay indoors for three days while the spraying occurred. Small planes flew throughout the region dropping what was referred to as "rodent napalm" across the land. In their wake, dump trucks and bulldozers roamed the streets to scoop up the rodent carcasses and then disinfect the roads and walkways. Unfortunately, there were many unanticipated casualties. Dogs and cats caught outside during the spray, native wildlife such as skinks, echidnas and even wallabies – pretty much everything in its wake was doomed.

One thing leads to the other, thought Lis. Over the following months, there were reports that soil was becoming almost lifeless. Farmers were up in arms. As was almost everybody. Some claimed it was the government's plan all along. Many had been too afraid to step outside their houses, let alone to demand accountability or action. Lis wondered if anything could be done anyway. The world as we once knew it was gone, maybe not forever, but for now. A certain amount of food was still being shipped into the region from other areas. That said, other regions had their fair share of problems as well. While here they had endless drought, to the south were catastrophic fires, up in Queensland and the Northern Territory, cyclones and flooding like never before. Multiple events all happening simultaneously. All material for Lissy's art projects of course.

It was a short jaunt to town and, fuel being unavailable of late, Lis slung her orange backpack over her shoulder and dangled a few polypropylene shopping bags from her hand. As she neared the supermarket, the small-leaf tamarind trees no longer wore leaves on their branches. Mere skeletons of their former selves. First the floods tested their hardiness and now with the return of El Niño, they were quite literally baked in hardened soil. Lis didn't know the names of most of the trees and they all kind of looked the same to her but this particular one she had often admired for the red fruits that dangled, three in a pod, like Christmas baubles bobbing from the branches. There was a beauty to the simplicity of the bare-bone remains, at least to her artistic eye. The trees fulfilled her love of the surreal juxtaposed on the tragic. She knew the forests were graveyards of their former richness but this too she had adjusted to. She saw it all through the lens of her camera as a phenomenon that sparked her creativity. Tweaked her drive to inspire awe. To capture the incredible. To make someone stop in their tracks at the beauty. Or, better yet, the horror, the terrible.

Lis was enjoying the stroll up and down the aisles with a trolley full of toilet paper, mince, a slew of veggies, bananas for the smoothies David had taken to making, and cultured vegan meat for Sal, who had stopped eating meat altogether. A commotion outside caught her attention and, as she lifted her eyes to the front window, she glimpsed the giant beetle-like buses rolling through town. Lis immediately gripped her phone and click-click, captured the sinister approach of the unknown vehicles, but soon enough the mounting frenzy roused her from this revery. Her mother always said she inhabited a dream world, that she resided in some other planet much of the time. This is real, a commanding voice urged in her mind. Not art. Get out of here. Run! Go home! David, Sal!

*\*\**

Sirens are blaring outside in the streets. The whole house is shaking. David can hear people screaming. He bounds down the stairs two at a time but, midway, terror stops him and he heads back upstairs to the front bedroom, Mum's room. The lights are off. He drops to his hands and knees and sprint-crawls to the front windows. He can hear shouts. He slowly edges himself upward on the sill so he can see outside. People are running in all directions through the street yelling "They're coming!"

David is not altogether surprised that this moment is here. He has been plagued by nightmares where he and his mates are rounded up, corralled, herded into enclosures, with tanks and men with guns in the streets. Although he is only thirteen, these persecution dreams have haunted him many a night. It's what you get with Jewish DNA, Dr Resnick, the shrink, explained to his mother. David remembers giving a shrug at the time as he doesn't know any other Jewish people. For a moment, he gives himself a shake as if to wake himself up. His fingernails dig into tight fists. This is really happening.

He peeks out the window for a few seconds at a time. There is a dark greenish-black bus-like vehicle moving slowly down the street. It has a black-and-white chequered design that stretches along where windows would normally be located. Men in black uniforms are in the street, gloved hands, masked faces, boots you wouldn't want to mess with. And guns, they have machine guns. He feels his heart beating rapidly.

David is paralysed for a moment, unsure of what his next move should be. Mum is not home and Sal slipped out, against the lockdown rules, to Lucy's place. He vaguely remembers Mum saying she was heading to the supermarket to pick up a few things. Should I go find them? That would be crazy-risky, he thinks, just as he hears the front door slam open and the loud clunk of steel-rimmed boots in the front hallway. He scans the room and decides quickly on a hiding place. Between the bed and the mattress. But that will look lumpy, he worries. He quickly pulls up the sheets, doona and pillows into a messy pile atop the bed. The red and purple roses on the doona mock the seriousness of the moment. He lifts the edge of the mattress up and crawls underneath it towards the middle of the base, face squeezed against the wooden slats towards the dusty floor. This is one time he is glad for his small size.

"Department of Public Health! Everybody out!" a voice blasts through a loudspeaker in the streets.

"This is a public safety announcement. You must leave now! Please board the nearest bus."

They are storming through the ground floor. Up the stairs now. At least two of them from what he can make out. They enter the bedroom. Closet doors banging open and shut.

Furniture is toppled. He feels the bed being lifted up. And then falling back down. His heart jumps in his chest with a jolt.

"Nobody here," calls a tinny voice.

"Move! Quick. Next house. Go, go," a staccato voice like a machine gun booms through the corridor.

He becomes aware that he is wet and trembling. He has pissed his pants. He anxiously wonders if he should have heeded these authorities. Perhaps he is not safe here like they say and he has made a huge mistake. His breathing begins to slow but he dares not move as he remembers the first rule of thumb in the emergency-planning school assembly: "Put your own air mask on first." Make yourself safe first. He lies still, not moving a muscle. He is alive, that's a start.

\*\*\*

It was too late for Lis to run home, to protect her children. Masked uniformed bodies, riot police, she thought, had stormed the shop and were grabbing everybody around her. She rushed down the aisle towards the back of the shop skidding to a stop when she heard a flash-bang and a smoky substance poured forth through the aisles. She could barely see the floor in front of her. She reached out to steady herself on a shelf, just as a rushing body smashed straight into her and knocked her to the ground. A searing sensation screeched through her body as a boot or maybe a high heel pierced her leg just above the kneecap and the pain and the panic around her ignited her into action. People everywhere running in all directions. Sirens. For a moment Picasso's horrific painting of the bombing of Guernica flashed through her mind and she needed to shake herself awake.

"Everybody, exit now. Come with us immediately. This is a health alert," a male computerised voice rang out in the shop and on the streets. "Please board the nearest vehicle. This is an evacuation. You must leave now."

Lissy's body protested. She, Gale and Sara had shared many conversations about this sort of thing in the past. Social breakdown, ecological collapse, military intervention. That was what this was, right? She was unsure. Lis was always the one to say, "But surely the government will protect us; they'll take care of us as best they can." Sara and Gale would snicker and shake their heads in disbelief as if she were incredibly naive. "What gives you that idea? Are they taking care of us now with their blah di blah di blah programs?" That is how it sounded to Lis. In one ear and out the other. Government policies, political jockeying, the news, not something that she cared to partake in. More of a local gal, with PTA, book club, a single mum raising her son and daughter, and relishing her artwork.

Gale and Sara's voices cut through loud and clear in her mind. "Hide! Don't let them get you. Then go home and hopefully David and Sal will be there waiting for you." She lowered herself to the dusty floor and crawled through the smoke until her outreached hands could feel the cold metal legs of a stand, one of the long metal refrigerated islands for the few fruits and veggies still sold: potatoes, onions, sometimes apples. There was a smallish-sized gap between the floor and the bottom shelf and, as she squeezed and pulled herself under, it reminded her of the feeling she got trying to pull on any of her pants of late. Her eyes were flooded with tears from the fumes. The pain in her leg. A blur. She was underneath now. The sound of boots quickly moving through the aisles. The male robot-like commands continued. People yelling. A baby crying. A woman shrieking. Somebody was being dragged past her. Lissy's eyes were shut but she could feel a body grazing against the shelving she hid under. She held her breath, grateful for her shawl as she pulled it up over her face mask and head to filter the air through the cotton fibres. She was in a cocoon now. Waiting for all this to pass. Ironically, she saw a painting in her mind of the faces of guards and people, and even hers now, transformed into rat faces, all of them hysterical and rushing around in every direction.

She began gasping for breath. The gas that had been sprayed constricted her lungs. It didn't make sense. They said they were rounding up people to keep them safe. Then they released a gas that was suffocating. She was crying now and pulled her shawl and the top of her smock tighter over her face. She let her hands explore the bottom of the stand she was lying under and the fingers on her right hand discovered an opening in the cool metal, a gap in the shelf just above her shoulder. Lis shifted herself around slightly to position herself where she could place her mouth over the opening in hopes of cleaner air. Her hands grasped the legs of the storage unit and, holding herself a few centimetres off the ground, she pulled her head up to the hole, slipped her shawl down for a moment and cupped her mouth around the opening, relieved to find uncontaminated albeit moist air to breathe. Her lungs sighed in relief as she gulped in a few mouthfuls of frigid air. The shouting was receding now, the sounds of boots and commands leaving the shop.

She dared not move. For a moment she glimpsed herself, five years old, frozen still as a sculpture in the cupboard when Dad was in a mood. That's what Mum would call it. A mood or sometimes a spell. Like a dark storm that swept in and overtook him. The cupboard was a place to stay safe until the storm passed and it was time to assess the damage. Her mother and her older brother, Will, keeping very still, and Bigby cowering in the corner or under the well-worn sofa, tongue protruding, panting. She heard her own breath now. She was the one gasping. The gas, smoke, whatever it was – chemistry had never been her strong point – started to ease up. She let herself slip back to the floor. Her eyelids checked the repercussions of opening. Painful, stinging, tearing up. She'd better wait a bit longer. She heard a child crying. It would be a young one to be here in the shop and not in quarantine at home. Her heart skipped a beat as she thought of David and Sal somewhere out there, hopefully hidden at home, waiting for her. As soon as she felt safe to get up, she would ring them both.

She waited and waited some more, not sure if she was safe yet. Her stinging eyes sent her back to a time when she and Will were playing hide'n'seek as children. Her big brother always found her in a few minutes flat and he would tease her no end about he being the almighty powerful one and she just a lowly subject who must submit to his authority. "I'm the king of the castle and you're the dirty rascal!" he would taunt in a sing-song voice. Clearly, their father's influence and too much unsupervised time spent playing Grand Theft Auto, an Xbox game of crime, violence, sex and drugs, not at all suitable for a 9-year-old. So this one time, 4-year-old Lissy decided to find a really clever hiding place as she wandered into the garage. Her eyes searched over the racks of dad's tools, hammers, screwdrivers and lots of other metal devices she did not know the names of. The white Hyundai sat squat in the middle of the concrete floor and when she heard Will calling out "ready or not, here I come!" she made a split-second decision to lie under the car itself. Against her better instincts. Dad wasn't home at the moment but she worried Mum would be mad if she knew. But how would she know? Usually if you weren't discovered, you ran out and touched the trunk of the Japanese maple tree on the front lawn of their brick suburban home. But this time she would hide until Will conceded and then come out. That was the plan.

Will had searched everywhere. He was big and strong for his age, while she was small, tiny for her age, like her mum had been. She could hear him stomping around the yard, the door of the garden shed squeaking shut. Then Will ran into the garage looking around the corners and behind the window frames that balanced against the back wall. "Lissy come on out, I give up, you win!" he finally called out but she decided to stay hidden a bit longer. A few more minutes to make up for all those times when he had found her in seconds and was mean to her. Becoming sleepy under the car, Lissy

32

daydreamed of the puppy she was hoping to get for Christmas that year. Even though her mother was something called Jewish, they still celebrated Christmas as that's what Dad's family did. Maybe she would call her new puppy Cottonpuff or Fluffball because surely it would be super soft and cuddly. Or maybe just something simple like Charlie. She liked that name, like that boy in school who always smiled shyly at her when they passed each other in the corridor.

Her thoughts had been interrupted by the sound of the car door slamming shut and the engine starting up. The garage door started coming to life and the car began to roll forwards. Lissy flung herself out from under the car and as she jumped up, her eyes locked on her mother's where an unforgettable look of horror flipped quickly to anger. Long story short, the day ended with her father washing her mouth out with a strong-smelling caustic soap and she spent the evening banished to her small bedroom, where she gazed out the window at the neighbourhood kids and Will playing kickball. Needless to say, a puppy did not eventuate that year.

The infant's cries startled her out of the memories that captivated her mind. It seemed like an hour had ticked by while Lissy's mind meandered down laneways of the past but perhaps it was only minutes. She no longer heard the rumble of trucks rolling down the street and the megaphone voices vaguely sounded in the distance. She was done waiting. She felt clear air on her breath once again but her eyelids were glued together. She slowly pried them open and was assaulted by biting sensations that sent them slamming shut once again.

She fluttered them butterfly fashion, flooding tears to flush out the residual toxins.

The child continued crying, its high-pitched wails bouncing off the walls of the shop. She was on the move now. After a slight pause to listen for any other sounds, Lis pulled her legs out from under the shelving and used her arms to slide the rest of her body out from underneath. A quick glance around in all directions. She didn't see anybody else. She took a moment to assess the damage to her throbbing thigh. There was a hole in her Thai pants and a bit of blood had soaked through but the skin was probably just a bit scraped and bruised. Covered in dust and dirt, she picked herself up off the floor, a bit unsteady on her feet for a moment, lightheaded.

She grabbed a bottle of coconut water on the shelf next to her, popped the lid off, gulped it down and discarded it on the floor. Her eyes scanned for her phone – it had been in her shopping trolley that she spotted lying on its side down the aisle. She headed towards it, relieved to find her mobile and quick-dialled David before realising there were no signal bars. No phone reception. She started moving quickly down the aisle, flinging grocery items into her backpack frantically as she made her way towards the door. Dry goods, she thought, more long-term storage items in case I can't go out for a while. The child's cries startled her again and she abruptly changed directions to head towards the shrill screams sounding from the back of the store.

There in a shopping trolley a toddler stood in the front section holding tightly to the push bar. The child had curly auburn hair loosely tumbling off her head like in an old-fashioned Shirley Temple photo. She was dressed in a tattered yellow frock with well-worn pink sneakers on her feet. She looked to be 2 or maybe 3 years old.

Lis moved towards the child and was about to pick her up when a voice in her head screamed at her to not play saviour right now. She was going to have her hands full as it was. Surely someone else would come back, the child's mother or aunty. Lis looked into the child's blue eyes. The girl stifled a sob and looked back at her.

"Sorry," Lis whispered and hurried off down the aisle, tossing flour, rice, legumes, and dried fruit into her shopping bags. She could hear Gale's snort as she tossed toothpaste in at the last minute. Lis was about to step out of the shop when the child's distressed wail reeled her back up the aisle against her better judgement. She picked the child up in one arm, her pack stuffed with groceries on her back, two laden shopping bags looped over her right arm, and departed from the shop.

She paused at the doorway and scanned the street. Nobody in sight. It was like a Sunday when the streets were bare. Not that long ago, everyone would be at home watching the footy, taking their children to sporting practice or perhaps sneaking a few pages of a book on the back verandah while cooking up dinner. She reminded herself again of the seriousness of this occasion. There had just been a forced round-up in her community. She seemed to be the only adult left at this moment and she must get home as soon as possible to find David and Sal. Her heart smashed against her chest as her children came to mind. A horrific image snapped into her mind of David and Sal lost in a sea of crying, terrified faces crowded into the black-box vehicles.

She headed through the door, laden with the weight of child and food, the throbbing from her thigh making her wince and at the last minute she threw her bags into an abandoned shopping trolley out front and thrust the child into the toddler seat. The girl's eyes opened wide and for the moment she was completely quiet as Lis wheeled the cart out into the middle of the street to head towards home. A voice in her head said she should go back inside and get more supplies but she urgently needed to get back to her children.

With the fuel shortages this past year the streets had become largely deserted as people had taken to bicycles and scooters, as well as the odd electric vehicle for those who had foresight and could afford their exorbitant price. Lissy's eyes took in a couple of abandoned cars in the street, a partly parked ute on the other side, a Suzuki in the middle of the street with its doors flung open, an array of bicycles lying randomly across the footpath and road.

She turned her head to the left and met the eye of a medium-sized golden retriever sitting quietly outside the shops, its leash attached to the bench. The dog was calm and tilted its head at Lis, offering her a series of hopeful tail wags. As she untied the retriever's leash from the post, she could hear Gale reprimanding her, saying she was always rescuing everybody, a baby and a dog added to her doomsday menagerie – not sensible, not useful – and yet her heart left her little choice. Practical was never her middle name.

She stood at the front of the shop by the wooden bench and empty taxi stand. An eerie silence blanketed the town. Lis straightened up for a moment to steel her nerves, then headed off, walking, not running, head stooped over, displaying a slight limp, as she pushed her cart accompanied by a small child in the seat and a dog who seemed to think nothing of joining in this posse. For the moment Lis was focused and clear, like when she was in the thick of a creative piece and knew exactly where she was going, what steps to take next, as if looking at a detailed map. It was only half a dozen blocks to her house but she ducked down one alleyway and then another in case there was any activity along the main streets. As she hurried past the Back Alley community art project, her eyes did not linger or even acknowledge the bold graffiti art that loomed over her from the brick walls of the 1950s buildings. Fortunately the child was enjoying the ride, the bumps and the speed. She clasped her little hands around the trolley bar and for now she did not seem to register that she had lost her mother. An image of David and Sal snapped into Lissy's mind and she picked up speed, smacking headfirst into a lean young man coming around the bend, dressed in trackies and a baseball cap. She noticed his black canvas sneakers, each foot pointing out in a vee shape firmly rooted to the concrete footpath.

"Hey, where is everybody?" he asked, looking slightly dazed.

"What?"

"Where are all the peeps? What's going on?"

"You missed it?" she said.

"Missed what?"

"Oh dear. Big black trucks rolled through town. Rounded everybody up. You'd better get some supplies real quick and head home."

"No way! Cool!" he said in disbelief looking down at the road, his head moving from left to right. And with that he turned around and headed towards the east end of town.

"Be careful!" she called out. Her heart was thumping now. The encounter had quickened her pace. Who knew what would happen if there were people running around and no law and order. She recalled that book she read last year, *Dry*, or something like that, set in California when the water in the taps stopped running. All chaos broke loose. Each person for themselves trying to survive, draining water from abandoned cars' windshield wiper tanks and wildly ransacking shops and houses. Order imploded rapidly with exponential force. She started running now. Running for her life. The child's cries only spurred her on, as did the dog at her feet. She limp-galloped towards home barely aware of the throbbing in her right thigh. This was an emergency like none other, not a dream, not a nightmare. This one was real; she knew it in her bones. And every second counted.

The shops, the street, the trees were all shapes in a blur like a camera sweeping quickly across a chase scene. Her eyes were on the child, the trolley and everything all at once, her peripheral vision and every sense functioning like never before. She lifted her head, scanned for signs of life, took in the objects abandoned on the road and footpaths: backpacks, handbags, bicycles, and a few steps ahead someone's abandoned grocery bag brimming with goods. In one smooth movement Lis reached down, grabbed it, and slung it into the trolley with Olympic speed. Further down the block, she recklessly smashed through a couple more abandoned shopping carts with her now full trolley.

Just one more block to the east and two to the north. Hurrying along. Last block. Lissy's eyes were on the houses to her right, their doors wide open, when she almost rolled her cart into a body lying across the side of the road. She was panting hard now. The dog, nonplussed, arrived first, and began a sniff check-up of the woman, who looked to be in her thirties, flat on her back, one arm slung up above her head and the rest of her body, clothed in jeans, T-shirt, sneakers, lying flat in corpse pose. The dog nuzzled the woman's head for a moment, gave her left cheek a slight nudge. No response. The retriever whimpered, then looked to Lis, who knelt next to the woman and picked up her wrist to feel for a pulse. Her own thump-thump heartbeat was so loud in her body that she couldn't tell. She shifted her fingers to the side of the neck and leaned over the woman to feel if there was any breath. Nothing, nothing, she muttered to herself.

"Gotta go!" she exclaimed aloud. Her voice gave her a start as she jumped up and veered around the body, with trolley, child and dog in gear for the last leg of the block to her home. As Lis rounded the corner to number 35, she saw that her front door, like the others on the street, was wide open. The garage too sat gaping. At this time of day, when the air started to cool, the neighbourhood usually came alive with households meeting from lawn to lawn or in little groups on the street itself. Today was different. Nobody in sight and, like the other roads she had travelled down, littered with discarded items, bicycles, cars with doors flung open, the odd gardening implement scattered across a lawn where someone was still hoping to eke out a flower or a lone potato in the parched soil. Number 35's front lawn was dry as always, bordered with some pretty succulents Lis had planted, odd shapes and sizes, one with pointy leaves and a delicate pink flower that she noticed even now.

The child began sobbing, tired or hungry or needing a change. Or perhaps they missed their mother. For a moment Lis felt horrified. She had taken another mother's child! And maybe their dog too! The dog wandered about zigzag style, lifting his leg every few metres or so to mark his territory on every corner of the yard. Lis shoved the trolley into the garage, picked up the child from the small seat and, loaded with supplies, headed into the house through the door inside the garage next to the neglected red Suzuki.

She raced inside her home and called out to David and Sal as she looked about wildly. Her cries of "David! Sal!" reverberated through the house. She hurriedly placed the toddler down on the circular amber rug in the lounge room, gathered some cushions and a blanket around the space hoping to keep the child nestled and, without losing a beat, raced up the stairs calling out her children's names, her voice pitched high in mounting alarm.

"David! Sal!"

Bursting into her bedroom, Lis thought she heard a muffled voice coming through the blankets from the messy bed. Her eyes darted over and she saw the mattress shifting slightly as David's beanpole legs emerged and then, as she rushed forward, the rest of him crawled out. She pulled him strongly into her embrace. She would never let him go.

"Mum, you're hurting me," he said.

She came to her senses. "Sorry David!"

She pried herself apart from her teenage son, hands on both sides of his head while she took a good look at him, smelly and soiled but intact. His eyes looked alert and present. He had always been good in an emergency. She remembered how cool he remained that time when he and Sal were trapped in an elevator. When the two of them were finally rescued, Sal was visibly shaken up. David was grinning as he recounted the stories he had told Sal to help keep her calm.

"David, where's Sal?"

"Not here. She's at Lucy's I think."

For a minute, Lissy's head clouded and began to swirl as she lost her footing.

"Mum, are you alright? Mum, you're bleeding!"

Lis was brought back by her son's voice. She looked down and saw the red smudge clotting the fabric of her Thai pants and sticking to her leg. Lis reassured David she was okay, it was nothing, and suggested that they both get themselves cleaned up. She needed a moment to think straight. At that moment, the toddler's cries burst through their bubble.

"Who's that?" David sounded alarmed.

They headed down the stairs as Lis began to tell her story to her son, or at least the bare outline, and as they neared the bottom of the steps, the dog came bolting into the house through the front door looking very pleased with himself. His tongue lolled out of his mouth, an infectious grin lightening the mood as the young child became distracted and started pointing and giggling, interacting with the new arrival.

A couple of hours passed and the afternoon sun painted the sky in gorgeous streaks of flaming red and orange hues. Lis, David, the child and dog were sitting on the well-worn sofa with Lis and David drinking red cherry drinks made from a powder Lis had stored in a tin in the pantry. The child used her fingers to eat mashed potatoes and fake meat balls made from a powder mix touted as the food of the twenty-first century. "Good for you, good for the planet" the advertisements proclaimed. Fortunately, Lis had a large tub of it; it would keep them going for a while. High protein, low fat. The child sat contentedly next to her furry companion. Although the girl must have been nearly three years of age, she had not yet uttered a word. David didn't speak much at that age either, especially with strangers, let alone in an unfamiliar house after a traumatic round-up that stole her mother away. Lis had tried the television for any news but, like their mobiles, there was nothing, no reception, nothing incoming, no connection to the outside world.

She was fixated on the front door for any activity. Still no sign of Sal. Lis began mentally planning to head out into the world once more in search of her daughter, who was hopefully holed up at Lucy's place just a dozen blocks away. The distance, normally a pleasant stroll, felt indomitable. She would wait a tad longer so she could use the cloak of darkness to stay hidden from any random people lurking around corners but, then again, perhaps the darkness would make her more vulnerable to attack. She decided to go in fifteen minutes' time. It was reassuring to hear the breath of the dog next to her. The child's cough brought Lis back to attention. Gosh, she hoped she hadn't brought the virus into the house.

"What shall we call the dog?" Lis asked, trying to sound casual.

"Wags," David replied.

"Wags it is."

As if on cue, Wags thumped his tail contentedly against Lissy's leg, his long mouth still smiling and drooling.

\*\*\*

It was time to head out. Lis had cleaned and bandaged the gash on her thigh and now donned lightweight tan trackies, sneakers and a linen hoodie. What she considered her most practical attire, the sort of clothing she normally only wore around the house. There was no more normal though, she sighed. And there hadn't been for quite some time. Children who were under constant stay-at-home orders, grocery shops with half-stocked shelves, peoples' movements in the community restricted to one day per week, masked up and required to check in on a government app wherever they went using wrist-tech, some state borders permanently shut long ago. Big Brother was certainly here now. Koalas extinct, soil devastated, forests burning, whole towns abandoned. She knew the story, yet somehow she and the kids managed to enjoy their slice of life. They had plenty of projects at home, creative ones, playful ones and, of course, home renovations. Add in the internet and devices with social media and streaming services. Yes, overall Lis, Sal and David had kept themselves busy and well. Sure, Sal had been pressing the boundaries of late, not unusual for her to sneak out to Lucy's. Then again, not unusual for Lis to duck out with Gale to the park down in South Lismore where they would have a chat and smoke a joint for old times' sake. Neither had seen Sara for close to a year now and Sara was not one to do online chats. Sara had her partner, Pot, with her though and they were both very competent out there in the bush. Lis knew that the time to head to the Meeting Place had now arrived; this was definitely the scenario she, Gale and Sara had been preparing for, a place to retreat to in case of emergency.

David pleaded with his mother to allow him to join her on her way to Lucy's but she insisted he stay home where he was safe for now and where he could watch over the child while she was gone. She decided to take Wags with her; maybe he could do more than smile if need be. Lis laced up her designer sneakers, slipped her thin hood over her head and went to the front door to survey the block.

'This way!" she called out and clapped for the dog to join her.

Wags trotted agreeably after her as she turned to the left, down the street, heading in the direction they had arrived from earlier. Remembering the body in the road she decided to wend her way, turning down Little Keen Street. It looked like her street at first glance. Doorways open, items discarded here and there.

Lucy's place was about half a kilometre away as the crow flies, somewhat longer via a series of left and right turns. Cutting across town in the silence of the abandoned streets, Lis could hear her heart pounding as she stealthily moved along the footpath. Her footsteps sounded booming to her ears. Wags was loving up the smells he encountered, lifting his leg on a series of trees and mailbox posts despite having only a drop or two of urine to spare for each. She hoped it was not a mistake to bring him along.

The street names flashed past as they moved from one block to the next – Zadoc, Bridge, Crown – then across the grassy island and the defunct railway tracks with only a couple more blocks to go south of the bridge that headed over the river and into town. They were just over the tracks when Wags and Lis in tandem spotted movement to their left by the bridge. Wags let out a bark as Lis spied the black truck parked at the junction, two uniformed figures standing alert on each end. Lis cried out to Wags and grabbed him by the collar, plopping down quickly in the high grass that surrounded the tracks. Shushing the dog, she lay still with Wags cradled in her arms, his low growls forming a nerve-wracking backdrop as they hid.

"Good boy. It's okay, shhhh …" she soothed.

For the second time that day, Lis found herself in hiding, alert and in a panic, afraid to move an inch. One step at a time, she coached herself, willing her mind to stay present. She half crawled, half dragged her round body along the grass, whisper-coaxing Wags to come along with her, firmly grasping his scruff. A few feet and she was panting, wishing she had stayed fit rather than blobbing out these past couple of years, but she was determined and began to imagine she was a soldier in Oliver Stone's *Platoon*, enemy fire all around her. She quickly tired of pulling herself forward and developed a rolling-pin movement, shifting her body like a skewer on a grill, from her back to her side, over to her front and so on. Another few minutes and she and Wags had reached the road on the other side of the tracks. She shifted herself into a crouch. Hardly a Ninja, she thought, but here I go. "One, two, three, go!" she whispered curtly to Wags and she swiftly sprang to her feet – well, perhaps more of a heavy clamouring movement – and lumbered across to the other side, out of sight of the guards.

Fortunately, there were no further close encounters as they rounded the corner to Lucy's place. The ghostly neighbourhood cloaked Lis in panic. It was bare. Barren. She scanned the desolate neighbourhood, its empty houses, open doors, no signs of life other than the odd dog roaming about here and there. It was starting to dawn on her that she might not find Sal, who was God knows where, a victim to the Round-up along with the rest of the neighbourhood. Lis strode along quickly now as she reached the last twenty metres to Lucy's place, where a young tabby splayed casually on the concrete landing by the front steps. Wags leaped gleefully towards the cat, who promptly landed a well-placed flick of her paw on his nose, engaging in get-to-know-you tactics. Lis wasted no time going through the open front door, calling out, "Sal! Lucy?" her voice bouncing off the walls like a ping-pong ball.

No response. No movement. Grating screeches of music drew her to the kitchen where a deep dish of nachos sat half eaten, two plates abandoned mid-Mexican binge. Her heart sank into quicksand at the sight of Sal's favourite carry bag, black with a red anarchist symbol on the back, slung over the wooden chair. And there on the marble laminate kitchen countertop was Sal's phone, clearly hers with its violet stars twinkling from it. Rage Against the Machine blared from the Bluetooth cube speaker next to it, rap metal, one of Sal's favourites. Much to Lissy's dismay.

"Killing in the name of, Killing in the name of."

Lis left the kitchen and raced through every room in the house calling out for Sal.

"Sal!" Distraught, Lis cried out once more with a wail that shook her body, her hands tightly fisted in the air, face scrunched up like an accordion as she crumpled to the floor overcome with grief, the truth sinking in with undeniable force. Sal was not to be found.

"Now you're under control. And now you do what they told ya."

After what felt like a lifetime but more likely a minute at most, Lis pulled herself up to the kitchen table and headed back through the lounge room and out the door, her eyes blinded by emotion, her feet moving of their own accord.

The journey back to the house was a blur. Lis and Wags stuck to the back alleys and crossed the tracks after the bend in Engine Street to avoid any encounters. Soon they were home, back with David and the child, the four of them once again sitting on the lounge while Lis considered what to do next. The electricity went out so they lit candles and placed them around the room. They were all hungry. But, when Lis went to boil up some easy pasta on her gas burner, she discovered that the town water tap was no longer flowing. No water, no electricity. Fortunately, there were still a couple of hundred litres in the rainwater tank so they could get by for now, but with this drought it would not last long.

As Lis drained the pasta, Wags jumped up with a growl to the sound of sirens piercing their eardrums. Lis ducked out to the front door and poked her head out. Searchlights roved the sky, a great yellow beam projected from the east, where she had seen the trucks parked earlier, and then another from the west. Her heart sank. They could be trapped in town. From her place there were only four roads leading out. She returned to the kitchen, opened a jar of spaghetti sauce and absentmindedly emptied it over the pasta. The four of them, Wags included, ate dinner in the lounge room. The child still had not uttered a word, yet she kept eyes on Wags and was content enough.

"Everybody in my bed tonight, David."

"Sure Mum," David replied rather quickly. "What about Sal?"

"Let's hope she's here by the morning."

"Do you think they got her too?"

"I don't know."

"I hope not." Her heart contracted with dread that Sal had been taken. But where? And by who?

They got into bed and the toddler started crying, calling for her mum. She had the sweetest little voice that broke Lissy's heart.

"Mummy? Mummy?"

"What's your name?" asked David.

Silence.

"My name's David," he said quietly. "What's yours?"

"Chloe," she whispered back and Lis cradled Chloe in her arms until they all nodded off together.

But Lis could not sleep. The sirens continued throughout the night and she anticipated the guards busting into their house at any minute. She lay awake plotting their escape. She considered the car. They could stash food and essentials in there – she did have an emergency canister of petrol (thank you Sara, you were right!) but this town only had so many ways in and out, with bridges to traverse, and she would not be surprised if all entrances were blocked off. What would Gale and Sara tell her to do now? She imagined herself walking right up to one of the men in black.

"Excuse me sir but I would like to leave town. Would you please let me through?"

Ridiculous, she thought. Absolutely pathetic. I have no idea what to do. For a moment she indulged in a fantasy featuring Lis the artist waltzing over and photographing these men in black, but fear triggered a flashback to her angry father, sending her spinning down the rabbit hole to her past. Five years old, hidden behind the door between the stairwell and the garage, her giant father shouting at her sobbing mother, looming over her, a glass grabbed from the benchtop

49

in his hand, the words a litany she did not understand, her mother with hands shielding her face and head, saying, "Luke, Luke take it easy, it won't happen again." Lissy, quiet as a mouse, frozen in time in the corner, until fast-forward, peeking out from behind the door, her mother and father both sobbing together on the blue-tiled kitchen floor, kissing each other, little Lissy trembling, taking this opportunity to sneak out of the room.

She had to figure a way out of this town and over to Sara's place or further on, to the Meeting Place. She would get up at first light and get ready with backpacks, supplies. She could do this. As she fell asleep Lis was half aware of Chloe coughing away through the night.

# 3    Sara

The music is thumping. Bodies gyrate under flashing neon lights of a dark smoky club. Sara is in her element, woozily moving to the beat, hips in full gear atop a circular podium at the front of the dance floor. Lithely grooving, fully zoned out. She drops to the floor and shimmies along between flailing arms and bodies to a metal pole that she fronts, grinding her pelvis into the hardness, in sync with the booming beat. She sports tight gold spandex shorts and a stretchy sleeve over her curvy breasts, along with tall leather boots. Wavy dark hair spills over her shoulders, across her face. A woman in leather shorts and vest sidles towards her and pushes herself into Sara's backside, gyrating sensually from behind. The room, engorged with bodies, starts spinning like a merry-go-round and Sara begins to lose her grip on the pole as a man grabs her, holds her forcefully, squeezes her unsuspecting breasts, moves his jeaned legs closer to her backside. She cries out as everything goes blurry. She tumbles back into her bed.

*** 

I wake up with a start and sit bolt upright, then fall back into my bed. I'm not sorry to see the details of the dream slip away into wisps of smoke. I know in my guts I've had another "violation" dream. They come in waves and I tend to snap awake when I am about to be penetrated, yet another crime perpetrated. My childhood haunts me no matter how many hours spent working at it in the psych's room – cognitive, analytic, somatic, hypnosis, gestalt. So many insights, so much sobbing, yet still it goes on. I am determined to make the effort pay off and one of these nights I'm going to stand up to the perp, lay into him once and for all. I've nicknamed this version of myself Ninja-Sa and, as I roll out of bed now, I set myself into Ninja warrior stance, exhale loudly, hands in tight fists, boxing arms at the ready.

"Ninja-Sa!" I call out my war cry. "Yahhhhhh!" My arms spring forward and cuff the imaginary opponent on his chin, nose, belly, my knee plunging mercilessly into his groin.

For a moment, I forget the argument that Pot and I had last night, one of many we've had these past few months while we have grown coolly apart. I've had a slew of lovers over the years and it looks like this one too will soon go by the wayside. I think Pot has reached their limits with me and my perpetual relationship dissatisfaction. I'm good at finding fault with Pot: their emotional unavailability, that slightly sarcastic tone of voice, the downturned mouth when we see each other at the end of the day. I want to walk into a room and see my partner's face light up like a beacon in an otherwise bleak world. Nobody can be present all the time but I like, I need, ongoing deep connection. Except when I don't of course. I am ridiculous, I know, but this is, in part, my trauma speaking. I want safety, intimacy, to be understood. I want what I want! I am once again with someone who needs a lot of space, is introverted, quiet and undemonstrative. Pot withdraws metaphorically to their cave much of the time. Literally as well. Like today there is no sign of Pot, who has probably gone out bush to harvest yams or to work on clearing a back track. We are both on tenterhooks in the final throes of our relationship.

My shoulders sag under these heavy thoughts. My love relationships are as brittle as the parched land. I am interrupted from my reverie as I hear the chop-chop of helicopters in the distance reminding me of the more dire circumstances we are in. After the 2026 Big Spray backfired, the Health Minister warned that the land would become unsafe to humans. Now, a couple of years later, we have been hearing helicopters in the distance and word has spread that people in the next valley have been removed from their land. A few weeks ago, we discovered a guard station erected where our road connects to the main road to town. Sinister-looking black armoured vehicles and guards shielded head to toe are stationed there. Those who decided to go check it out more closely have not been seen since. At the same time, satellite internet went down, and telephone reception has been non-existent here for years now.

Despite these circumstances, we have fared quite well here in Barkers Vale, with food and medicine swaps, street gatherings and meetings to discuss strategies for protecting ourselves and our loved ones. Living in a rural region has always been a refuge from regular society. A gap we find in the rocks. A crawl space in a calamitous time.

The sound of helicopters draws closer. I peek outside our small wood cabin and a couple of the choppers land not that far from where I stand. I spot a half dozen fully helmeted figures in bulky black gear, covered head to toe, no faces visible as they dismount from the aircraft. Daunting to say the least; Darth Vader comes to mind. They beeline in pairs towards Zack and Tilly's place, Linda's and then Tom's, accompanied by sinewy German shepherds who bark excitedly as they race towards the houses. I open the back screen door and yell out to Pot over the sound of the helicopters' whirr. No sign of Pot. One more helicopter lands. My place will be next.

I grab my red backpack, prepped in advance for just this sort of occasion, and lumber down the hill past a patch of scrubby lantana where I turn the corner and duck under the bushes to the hidden track. I am rather large for my 170-centimetre stature but, at thirty-four years of age, I am also strong bodied from life on the land and can move with speed when need be. I readjust the straps on my pack and stride down the familiar twists and bends of the path, putting as much space and time between me and what I have called home for the past fifteen years. When I arrive at the creek, now a mostly dry rock bed, I am tempted to crawl into the hollow of the majestic ancient strangler fig but a single loud gunshot convinces me to keep moving, climbing past the quandong trees and through the lawyer vine into the darkness of the rainforest beyond. A lone cane toad, oddly poised on the forest floor where a drop or two of water can still be found at dawn, catches my eye. Never seen them down here before, but nothing is the same anymore. Frogs are rarely to be found. My stomach plummets to my feet with the helicopters circling the valley overhead as I make my way up the ridge, scrambling over rocks and under vines, hustling along, my breath laboured.

It takes me about ninety minutes to arrive at what my friends, Gale and Lis, and I mundanely call the Meeting Place, a designated site that we prepped in case of a state of emergency. The three of us are old friends, with Gale and my friendship dating back to high school. Lis joined us about ten years ago, making us into more of a gang. We three have knocked around together ever since, going to concerts and movies together, dinners at the Thai, Indian, Mexican or just pub fare at the Tatt's when it used to be open. A couple of beers, a nice meal, maybe a smoke back at Gale's later. This all changed when Gale and Lis coupled up with partners, and eventually two children in Lissy's case and one in Gale's, but we have still found the time through the years to meet up on my creaky verandah now and then with a cuppa and a little tour of the garden or at one of Lissy's art openings in town at the regional gallery.

The three of us. We steeped ourselves in many a conversation on "how to prepare for inevitable social collapse" and "what to do when the apocalypse hits".

"It's like being back in the Old Testament!" I've joked to them on occasion, although I admit I tend to be the only one laughing. My tongue rolls easily off words like doomsday, disaster, catastrophe, cataclysm, collapse. That said, I am dead serious about these matters. I often initiate conversations that are not for the fainthearted. Will ecological disaster strike first or civil unrest? A military coup?

I was most certainly not laughing when the fires came roaring through the bush in 2019. There was a moment when Gale and I locked eyes, Gale's face stony, only the muscles around her eyes betraying her steely emotions. Mine, of course, were flowing with tears. We were terrified by the ash that floated down and the smoky skies that loomed day and night both here at the edge of the Border Ranges as well as in Ballina and Lismore, where Gale and Lis live.

"I always thought we could retreat to the bush," I bemoaned. "I just assumed we would at least be safe there." I tried not to cry.

"We can't assume anything," Gale responded, always the super-practical one. Dispassionate even.

This became our motto. We can't assume anything. We can hoard survival food. We can build a bunker. We can plan for evacuation. But, who knows, maybe aliens will land on the planet and take over. In fact, our friend Amy believes this is the case, that reptiles are in charge now, hastening the warming of the planet so they can comfortably spread and multiply. A bit far-fetched perhaps but all of us, even Lis, could see how things have gone haywire with the weather, just as scientists predicted several decades ago.

"It's like we're characters in our own dystopian novel!" Lis would muse, always viewing life through a creative lens, potential material for her next photographic exhibition. I blatantly ignored comments like this.

"Being prepared in whatever ways we can is a good idea," I remarked. For me it was a real thing, and I considered myself a budding bush survivalist having just finished a course on emergency wilderness first aid and another on medicinal plants. After much trial and error, I had finally mastered the art of starting a fire with a couple of sticks and some dry balled-up moss as kindling.

"Let's find a place in the bush with fresh water, somewhere obscure enough that we are safe as well," said Gale. "If we pick a place like Rocky Creek Dam, everybody will be there. Too obvious!"

"As long as the forests aren't burning," I lamented. "The rainforest should be safer, hopefully."

Eventually we arrived at our solution. If Lismore was still safe and friendly, we would meet at Lissy's house, just outside the centre of town. If town wasn't safe, we would meet at my property in Barkers Vale, an hour away. And, if that wasn't safe, we would meet up at Leicester Creek and into the Border Ranges at the Meeting Place.

A couple of years ago, in 2026, I guided Lis and Gale up the creek from my place to a rivulet that still boasted a sparkling waterfall and a delicious basin to dip in. Lis went into *Star Trek* mode, saying this was "first contact" with this special place. I called to the Ancestors and announced our greetings and our names aloud. There, under a lofty teak tree and a blue quandong, we created a small hideaway with a tarp and a small platform up in the quandong. We gathered a variety of veggie seeds – mustard greens, pumpkin, zucchini, cucumber – and put these in a sealed metal chest. I was in my element, a mission is always good for my mood, so I took great pleasure in spiffing the place up. Various tools – knives, lighters and matches, the sorts of things you find in an "End-of-the-World" survival guide – were collected and stored, then camouflaged with lantana branches interwoven with

Bangalow fronds and random-looking forest detritus. Quite a good job, if I don't say so myself!

That last time the three of us were at the Meeting Place was over two years ago now. While there, we were hit by the last big rainfall I can recall and we were keeping dry under the tarp, admiring the little log stools and woven storage baskets we had made. Giddy with excitement, the unknown looming just beyond grasp.

"What about water? Should we store water?" Gale was on task as always. She was speaking loudly over the sound of the rushing water we were standing next to.

"Why would we do that?" Lis laughed. "It's all around us."

"Drought!" Gale and I exclaimed in unison.

"Or what if the water became toxic?" I said, ever the doom-and-gloom one of the trio. I enjoyed this role. "What if chemicals have been poured into every creek in the country and drinking it causes instant death?"

Lis laughed loudly, no doubt seeing images in her mind for the "Dystopia in Motion" exhibition she was developing. When Gale and I did not join in her glee, the sound of her laughter faded away into the creek, replaced by a rare sobering moment of silence. We all nodded our heads in agreement and, when I returned the following week, I brought half a dozen 25-litre containers to fill with creek water along with water purification tablets. These I hid in the bush, in a little area between some rocks not 10 metres from the platform.

Gale, Pot and I last met at the Meeting Place in June 2026; Lis was off being busy with some creative thingo. It was still somewhat wet then. Now, two years later, everything is mostly dry.

I arrive at the Meeting Place and wait there for a couple of days for Pot to arrive. With no sign of Pot or Lis or Gale, I head back to our land, where I crouch anxiously in the nearby bush until I am sure the helicopters and men have left. I return home and there is no sign of Pot or any of the neighbours. I continue to hold a slight glimmer of hope over the next few days but I have a sinking feeling that the Authorities have taken everyone from our valley, including Pot, to wherever they took all the others.

Now I am the only one left. As far as I know.

# Part 2 Round-up Week 1

## June 2028

# 4    Gale

"Good morning friends."

She awoke to what sounded like a familiar digital voice, used in phones across the globe. For a moment she was comforted. The voice that had guided her when she was lost while driving in big cities, that told her a joke when she was lonely, that conveniently recorded and sent a message for her when she was driving. Gale's eyes opened and looked up to the far-right side of the block, where a small speaker was built into the ceiling. What sort of game are you playing? she wondered, alarm tightening in her chest.

"In a moment you will hear three tones and a green light will blink by the conveyor. A tray will slide through the small window. Take the tray. You will have fifteen minutes to eat your food. When you hear the tones again, please replace your tray on the shelf before the screen slides shut. If you do not replace your tray, you will not receive a new one at the next mealtime. This message will not be repeated. Thank you for your attention."

Three tones sounded. Like elevator harmonies announcing one's arrival at the selected floor of a modern building. Pleasant sounds. A rather polite message. Perhaps things were not as bleak as she thought. The throbbing in her left wrist dispelled this thought as she applied pressure to it with her right hand. Gale looked up at the small round grate in the corner of the ceiling that was the speaker. Next to it was what looked like an eye of sorts, a small shiny round object like a toy flying saucer mounted well out of reach. A camera no doubt. Somebody out there was watching. Recording her every move.

The tray arrived through the metal portal, a small door sliding up smoothly. It was a double door with a cavity between, just large enough for the brown plastic tray and its contents. Gale sensed some movement on the other side, perhaps the delivery person, one of the guards, but she was unsure. Gale quickly grabbed the cafeteria-style tray off the shelf and carried it to the metal chair and small table bolted to the concrete floor and the wall next to the bed. Gale slipped onto the seat. Her legs dangled; the furniture was obviously not made for someone of her modest size. For a second, she swung her legs back and forth like a young person. She then settled on a cross-legged sitting position while she examined the contents of the tray.

A bowl filled with a mound of barely warmed pink and brown slop reminded her of what they used to call mystery meat at the high school cafeteria. Perhaps cultured meat from animal cells. Although she had never tasted it, lab-cultured meat had recently become quite commonplace at McDonald's and other fast-food joints. Or perhaps it was dog food or literally dog meat. Gale felt her stomach turn over.

She picked up the metal spoon and tested the contents, closing her eyes as the food slid into her mouth. Bland and a bit off-putting, she forced herself to swallow. She needed to keep her strength up. She would eat what they gave her, do what they asked. For now. Observe. She knew how to do this. Like mapping out a financial system. First learn about the idiosyncrasies and then think outside the box, come up with a clever solution. Patient and persistent. Lis always said she was like a dog with a bone, not one to give up.

After the meal, if you could call it that, she took a further look around. She paced the cell that at best was 2.5 by 2.5 metres. A perfect square. She felt dizzy and momentarily leaned forward with hands on knees. Then, looking up at the ceiling, she noticed the large globe was emitting a yellowish glow that reminded her of the sun. She visualised the sun rising and setting each day until her head had cleared.

Gale continued to appraise her surroundings. The bed frame was metal and heavy, immovable, tightly bolted to the floor. The mattress, or what passed for a mattress, was more like a thin yoga mat that could be shifted from the bed to other parts of the cell. She tried it out in every corner, sat on it, lay on it, folded it up against the wall, punched at it for a moment. Then she rolled it up under her head as a cushion while she sprawled on the concrete floor, positioned to catch the weak rays of light from the globe on her face. The closest thing to a moment of pleasure.

A day passed. Two meals and soon the light blinked out. And another day. She spent the time in a slumber, heavy and tired no matter how much she slept in her concrete block. The underside of her wrist was threatening infection, swelling up, throbbing. The hours stretched by interminably. She lay on her back and rested her knees on the roll. She had never been one for stillness and by the third day she was crawling out of her skin. She did a few sets of prisoner squats, hands laced together behind her head as she mulled over her situation. She was jumpy and spent hours pacing her cell, thoughts ricocheting back and forth in her mind. She recalled the medic saying they were in quarantine. She could see the slogans displayed at the front of the facility. "For the Good of the All" and "Keeping Our Communities Safe!" She relived events of a few days ago, a video zooming along on fast forward through her mind, her heart racing alongside to keep up. Anxiety was her usual go-to and she knew her brain was different from the norm, but this was something new. Her amygdala was sounding its alarm incessantly like an all-hours watchtower. She thought of Toby, how he would have been hysterical when she did not come home three nights ago. She remembered him pacing at the kennel that time, whining, tongue frothing, when she went to pick him up after leaving him there for a couple of nights. She felt sick thinking about what might have happened to him. She would give anything to be throwing a stick for him on a Ballina beach walk.

On the morning of the fourth day, the warm digitised female voice spoke just after the breakfast tray had been removed.

"Good morning number 87."

Gale looked up in surprise. A personal communication! That was the number on her door. Eighth floor, seventh door, from what she could tell. She stood up and looked up to the eye in the ceiling.

"Hello? Who are you?" she called up to the ceiling.

"How are you feeling today 87?"

She paused, uncertain.

"My wrist is hurting where the wrist-tech was installed."

"Thank you. That will be all 87."

The ensuing silence punctuated Gale's desperation.

"Wait!" she called out. "What is happening here, what do you want from us?"

***

The next morning there was a break in the usual schedule. The voice announced a three-minute shower. Above the water tap was a round shower head in the ceiling. Gale quickly removed her clothing and positioned herself under the tepid water that sprinkled down. It was like being washed in detergent, no softener, no towels. Gale felt mildly cooler. Although there was a slight whirring of air from a built-in vent, the cell was still dense with heat.

The hours passed. Gale sat. Gale thought. The walls were closing in on her, her heart pounding as she tried to sit still. Thoughts sparked explosively, her neural activity igniting like a firing range. She paced. That was better. Images floated in all directions in her mind. She took some comfort thinking about that time she and Sara were at the Three Sisters in the Blue Mountains – a rare moment of silence as the two sat quietly, in awe, peaceful. Now she felt agitated, more than agitated, she was spinning out of control. Her wrist was throbbing, her mind was whirling endlessly and she was feeling hungry. The two meals each day were too small and barely edible.

The days went by in a blur. She would have lost all sense of time except that each day, after the morning meal, she dipped her finger into the lukewarm drink, a slimy, bitter affair, stood atop the little metal table that was affixed to the wall, reached up and marked a line on the wall overhead. Prisoner fashion. She had seen this many times in films over the years.

It was her seventh day in the cell when the voice broke through the silence after the morning meal.

"In a moment your door will open. Please move into the corridor for an exercise session."

Gale did as she was told, relieved for a moment to be leaving the confines of the four walls. Out in the hallway, she could see female robo-guards stationed at the corners.

"Please proceed to walk clockwise in single file. Do not attempt to communicate with one another. Keep your eyes on the ground in front of you. Do not look at other residents. There will be consequences if you deviate."

Gale stood behind the woman in the next cell, number 88. She could see the tension in the younger woman's shoulders. The woman's dark hair hung long and tangled. She could see two other women in front of her neighbour, an older woman further on, a heavier woman further yet. She knew there were two others behind her as well, five along her side of the floor and presumably five others directly opposite. Her mind mapped out the locations as if to create a scaffold to stabilise her nervous system.

"You will hear the steady pulse of a metronome. Please move your body in time with the beat. Do not break formation or your wrist-tech will promptly inhibit you. You will walk for twenty minutes. If you are unable, please return to your room by scanning your wrist-tech when you arrive at your doorway. Do not speak to anyone! Begin now."

The first five minutes passed in a heavy silence as the women cautiously moved around the corridor as instructed. It felt good to Gale to move her body and to be out of her cell. The beat gradually increased its pace and Gale's legs responded positively. She felt faint for a moment but held on and continued to move.

Another five minutes or so and the heavier woman several down the line returned to her cell. The others continued.

"What's to become of us?" cried a woman from the other side of the floor. "We need to get out of here!"

No one dared to reply and, as Gale turned the bend, she could see the woman collapsed on the floor. The woman remained there for most of the remainder of the session. In the last round, she returned to her feet and to her cell along with the rest of them. There was no further talk, no attempts to escape.

Back in her cell, Gale meticulously turned over the details of her situation, looking for a clue, a way to get herself out. Uncertainty gnawed at her with a voracious appetite. There were times in the day when she took to the bed, knees to chest. At others, she sat on her mattress in the corner of the cell, immobilised. There was nothing to distract, nothing to take her mind away from the desperation that oozed through her pores, the growing ache in her wrist.

The first rays of morning light brightened Lissy's thoughts as she pictured Sal loping through the doorway, the four of them sitting down at the breakfast nook and heartily chomping pancakes, Wags at their feet thumping his tail insistently to remind them to drop a piece or two for him. She pictured herself heading out the door into the sunshine to greet her neighbours across the way, an air of normality gracing the street.

Chloe's cries startled Lis out of her reverie.

"Ma! Mummy!" Chloe wailed as Lis pulled her into her arms and proceeded down the hallway to the stairs. David jumped up too and followed her, his blue alligator blanket trailing along the floor.

"Mum, what are we going to do?"

Lis didn't know how to respond. She could soothe him, tell him everything was going to be fine. She could say they needed to figure out a way to get out of town and head to Sara's. She had never been very practical. She had no idea how they were going to get out of here and she felt heavy with fear that Sal was nowhere to be found and they were surrounded by masked guards posted throughout the town. She could focus on getting breakfast together – yes, that was a good idea.

She murmured to Chloe as she gave David's shoulder a squeeze with her spare hand.

"How about you see if we have any pancake mix and we can fix up some yummy animal shapes for breakfast and then we'll figure things out from there."

That sounded good to her ears and David, taking her cue, charged down the stairs eagerly. He always liked to have a mission and she could count on him to have a level head. He certainly didn't get this calmness from her and she was grateful for it today, managing a small smile as he leapt down the last two stairs and scooted right towards the kitchen.

David had always had a knack with young children and as she fried up the pancakes in the skillet with a bit of oil – no butter these days – David devised a little game of peek-a-boo to amuse Chloe. He picked up pots and pans, plates and mugs, and hid his face behind them only to reappear with a range of comical faces and gestures until Chloe and he dissolved into waves of belly giggles and squeals that filled the kitchen with a joy that camouflaged their dire predicament. Wags ran around barking, jumping and egging both children on, fully absorbed in the playtime. Only Lis was a million miles away, dreaming and waiting for a plan to magically incubate in her mind.

She landed on a time when Gale and Sara were drinking shots of tequila as they played "What happens after the apocalypse". It was one of those conversations that popped up repeatedly, an ongoing series of reiterative reflections on a myriad of doomsday scenarios that could put an end to life as they knew it. Be it environmental, social, economic or political collapse, what was clear to both Gale and Sara was that humanity, along with many others, sat precariously perched on the edge of imminent disaster, no matter which angle you looked at things from.

Lis went along for the ride. It inspired her creative impulses and gave her the impetus to explore the edges of civilisation, the cracks, the holes, the fragility of social order, through photographic and multimedia exhibitions. Now she was wishing she had paid more attention as she tried to remember what had been said about the military takeover scenario that she was sure had been discussed. She let something arise in her mind that approximated her memory.

"Ok, Gale and Lis, what if you're at home and the fascists roll into town Gestapo style?" This would be a typical "apocalypse" opener question from Sara who was always game to play after a quick shot or two.

"Hide?" suggested Lis. "We could have a bunker!"

"I definitely could not live holed up in a cellar," Gale commented. "Maybe we run?"

"I reckon we meet in the bush," said Sara. "But first you would have to figure out how to leave town without falling into the military or whoever's hands."

"Easy for you to say since you live in the bush!" Lis said.

"No way we can plan that now," she remembered Gale saying. Very sensible.

"I don't even want to think about this," Lis countered.

"Well, you have to," Sara insisted.

"What are the chances I would survive?" Lis bemoaned. "Surely you two, but not me. I'd probably be the first one taken down, merrily absorbed in some piece I'm working on, music blaring. I would barely notice they'd rolled into town, until I was completely ambushed."

"Just in case then," Sara murmured. "Use that imagination of yours for a moment."

"You've got more smarts than you let on," Gale quipped.

"Yeh okay, so we pack things up, leave unannounced and sneak out."

Their voices blended from here in a chorus.

"Through the parks."

"Look for anyone else who might be an ally."

"Watch out for crazy people who are going to sabotage your exit."

"Dress to blend – not your usual purples or reds Lissy."

"Listen to David. He's got good sense."

"Keep clear of the bridges."

"But look underneath. Go under, not over the bridges."

"Follow the rivers."

And then she heard what she was looking for.

"Try the wooded areas in the parks to weave your way down to South End … try the river under the bridge, there's a track there where mob usually hang out … I would start there."

"Keep your wits."

"Don't give up."

"Mum! Mum! The pancakes are going to burn!"

Lis came to in a rush. She had vacated the kitchen in her daydream but she had found what she was looking for.

"Here you go," she said as she flipped rhinos, elephants, bears and cows out of the pan and onto a plate in the centre of the orange lino-topped kitchen table.

"Eat up cos after breakfast we're off!"

\*\*\*

What to bring, what to pack up? Stick to essentials. Chloe was crying almost non-stop this morning in what felt like a painfully slow scene from an action horror flick. Lis felt like she was lugging a heavy sack of rice around the house as she straddled Chloe on her hip while trying to figure out what to take with them. Any minute now, the guards could come rushing in the front door, alerted by Chloe's shrieks. Chloe was understandably upset – her mother was nowhere in sight and she'd been abruptly shacked up with strangers, urgently preparing to flee town.

Lis breathed a sigh of relief as Wags came to the rescue with Pink Dolly in his mouth, one of Sal's raggedy favourites that she had hung onto from childhood. The doll was somewhat worse for wear yet still had a twinkle in her little button eyes. Wags nudged his cold nose against Chloe's leg as Lis leaned into her closet looking for a backpack or something she could put Chloe in so she could move around unhampered. The retriever caught Chloe's attention and, to Lissy's relief, she was able to put Chloe down on the carpet. Next thing the little one was toddle-racing after Wags into Sal's room, where there were plenty more dolls waiting to be played with. Although Sal was tough and a rebel, she had a softness to her and was sentimental about her old travelling companions. Lissy's heart sank as she thought of Sal. She would find her, wherever they had taken her.

"Mum, are you ready to go?"

David burst into the room, a medium-sized backpack slung over his shoulders, a cap on his head, sporting a dark-blue lightweight hoodie, jeans and sneakers. Lissy's heart warmed at the sight of her dear sensible son. She needed to keep him safe at all costs, and this new little child as well. A large backpack that she could partially fill and stick Chloe in the top? No, that would certainly not work.

"Mum. How about we use this for Chloe?"

David held the perfect toddler carrier backpack in his small hands.

"Where did you get that?"

"I went across the way to the Robinson's house. Pascal is about the same size as Chloe."

"David, it's dangerous out there!"

"I was careful Mum. I looked around first, nobody in sight, then scooted across like they do on—"

"Okay but don't go out again until we're ready. You packed your toothbrush?"

"Yes, Mum," David groaned.

They finally made it out the door. The four of them. Lissy in her attempt to be practical was still in attire that oozed artist, with purples and turquoise colours woven into her South American poncho that she would shortly take off as it was too hot to wear it anyway. David had removed his hoodie as well and mimicked Luke Cage in a Marvel flick, with a yellow T-shirt to seal the deal. Chloe remained in the same flowered frock and pink sneakers. And then there was Wags, being himself with his good nature and energetic bouncy gait, tail swiping back and forth like windshield wipers.

Chloe sat in the carrier that Lis had hooked onto her nylon backpack, stuffed haphazardly with easily dispensed food – cereal, nuts, oats and pasta, along with an old spirit cooker she found in the garage on their way out. She also grabbed the first aid kit and a few bottles of water that they could hopefully refill along their way. That was about all she could really manage to put on her back and still be able to walk easily. One spare blouse, a family photo with her, Mike, Sal and David.

Unlike his mother, David had packed his torch, Swiss Army Knife, a map of the region, aspirin and Panadol, paper and pen, a spare T-shirt and shorts, his Mp3 player with music and earbuds. He thought for a moment and then added in some rope, candles, a lighter and toilet paper. He still had room in his backpack, even though it was small like him, and as they left the house he dashed into the kitchen and grabbed whatever else he could from the pantry. David was fully in his element; his life had just become his very own make-your-own-ending comic book. Adrenalin was pumping and he was trying not to grin from ear to ear as he knew this was a serious situation.

Just as they were about to leave, Lis raced back into the house and found a pen and paper to write a quick note to Sal. She kicked herself for almost forgetting to do so. What was she thinking?! She let Sal know they were headed out to Sara's place and would come back to get her once it was safe to do so. Please wait here for us! She silently prayed that Sal would be back soon enough.

Rejoining the others, a motley crew they were as they headed down the street, ducking through side roads and sticking to the smallest arteries as they made their way to the main road that would take them out of town north-west towards Sara's land and the national park where they had their secret Meeting Place set up.

As they approached the roundabout at the bridge out of town, they slowed their pace, not that they had been moving all that fast. They could see a guard station up ahead with black vehicles and at least one uniformed and helmeted guard moving back and forth. Like Buckingham Palace, Lis thought. While Lis momentarily lost herself in dreams of holidays to Europe, David scanned below the bridge to where he caught the eye of an older Aboriginal man who stood facing them.

"Mum, look!"

Lis lowered her head and was about to call out to the man when he subtly shook his head and put a finger to his lips. He raised his hand to indicate that they should stop where they were and with his eyes pointed towards the old, elevated train tracks, showing them that they should head there. The railway system, disused for decades now, did indeed offer an alternative way out of town and clearly the way they were headed along the road was heavily guarded. They wouldn't stand a chance.

David raised his hand and gave the thumbs up as they headed towards the bank where the tracks were. They were able to walk alongside the tracks for about 30 metres or so.

"Lucky we saw him, eh Mum?"

But Lis was miles away. She was reliving that time when Aunt Lolly told her that a number of generations back, before the Second World War, when Jews like her were being deported by rail to killing centres in German-occupied Poland, her great-great-grandfather, or something like that, was an infant passed from hand to hand through the window of a train into the arms of a young couple who had witnessed the round-up and were horrified by the—

"Mum, we need to go on the tracks now."

David was right. The bank fell away on both sides and they proceeded to walk on the railway sleepers as the track rose to cross what remained of the river below. The river was not very wide and, once they were across, there was a park they could cut through that would land them at the edge of town. Right where they wanted to be.

David led the way, with Wags taking up the rear. They were a good 6 metres off the ground and needed to carefully step from one sleeper to the next, avoiding the small gaps in between.

"Doggy!"

Chloe let out a wail that stopped them in their tracks. They looked back and Wags was no longer behind them. They followed where Chloe's chubby little arm pointed downward and could see Wags heading towards the soccer field beyond. Of course, she thought, hopping from one sleeper to the next up here off the ground might have been a bit tricky for the four-legged creature.

There was nothing to be done.

Chloe's cries were starting to pick up in pitch and volume. Lis paused and, with David's help, she took Chloe out of the backpack and into her arms as they continued. With one eye trained towards the child, she murmured soothingly while her other eye was glued to the tracks, carefully placing one shaky foot in front of the other. Lis tried not to look between the sleepers to the mostly rocky banks of the river below. Hundreds of years ago settlers in the region logged the majestic cedars and used this river to float the logs downstream to the mill. Red gold they called it.

"Mum, look out!" David stopped and turned around to face Lis who was about to put her foot down where a sleeper was missing.

"I see it, David," Lis said, a slight quiver in her voice as she realised she had been daydreaming her way to a serious fall.

Now with her focus firmly on the tracks, she noticed Wags crossing the dry creek bed below them. Arriving at a stretch where the rotting sleepers had fallen away, they stopped dead. There was no going back from here but Lis was not sure how she and Chloe were going to get across this section. A knowing glance passed between mother and son; at the best of times Lis was clumsy and uncoordinated, not a picture of steadiness and balance. They stopped to confer. The gap was about 2 metres. David could get over no problem, like a tightrope walker on the rails. He had plenty of practice with a ratchet strap that he had strung in the backyard between the porch and the gum tree. This was right up his alley. Then maybe they could get Lissy's backpack and Chloe over to him.

"You should let me take Chloe across," David urged.

"David, you're too small. She weighs a bit."

"I can handle it, Mum."

"But if you lose your step …"

"I won't."

"At least give me your backpack; I can stuff it in the top of mine."

"Okay," David concurred.

So it was decided. Lis had to concede. Even though this seemed like a dangerous option, she had no idea how she was even going to get herself across without tumbling down to the hard rocks below. David took Chloe in his arms and stood for a moment gathering his wits about him. Before Lis had time to think, he had practically floated across the rail to the other side of the gap. His left foot slipped slightly towards the last of the open rail section but he managed to arrive safely.

"See Mum!" he said with a grin. "Just like on *Ninja Warrior*!" he cried out exuberantly. His favourite show, he watched it religiously, glued to the screen, hoping that one day it would be him up there challenged by obstacles of every size and shape. A small guy like him had some advantages when swinging through the air.

The challenge of getting Lis over still remained. This was in no way her strength. The steel runner was wider than her foot but Lis could feel her heart thumping dramatically as she looked down to the drop below the rails.

"I have rope," said David.

"Rope?"

"We could wind it around your waist and tie it down to the rails here. Like a safety rope. You could hold onto it."

"I don't know that it will hold me." Lis could feel her knees already shaking and she had not taken a step.

"I got some good knots."

"Have."

"What?"

"I *have* some good knots."

And with that David sat with Chloe on his lap atop the rails while he unwound the rope, tied it to the solid rail and flung the other end over to Lis. Shortly, she had hitched it around her waist, ready to take a tentative first step, using the rope to steady herself.

"You would make a good sailor, David."

"Or a climber. Or, even better, someone who rescues people and cats from up trees and rooftops."

A lone tear slipped down Lissy's cheek. She was terrified as she placed one foot in front of the other. She was almost halfway across after a few steps when she paused and looked down.

"Mum, don't look down."

But it was too late. Lis froze, her heart pounding in her ears, her legs shaking, her whole body trembling. She started to bend down.

"Mum, don't sit down!"

Too late again. Lis had manoeuvred herself to a sitting position, sideways on the suspended rail, her legs dangling.

"I'm stuck David." Lis felt her cheeks reddening, her head spinning. For a moment she was transported to that time her family drove for hours to Thredbo for a taste of winter skiing, a mountain that made its own snow all year round. The heavy silence in the SUV as they arrived at the resort was offset by the thrill of putting on the equipment: skis, ski boots, thermals, hats and gloves, all decked out and ready for the adventure, time to conquer the mountain. Then, just as they were about to head up the mountain, a barbed conversation between her parents about the room key.

"You two go ahead," her mother said in that restrained tone reserved for just such an occasion. "Will, take care of your sister."

Her big brother had been to the slope at least twice before, he had been to ski camp the previous year so he was familiar with the workings. With his help, Lissy got her equipment on and they joined the chairlift queue, Lissy working her little legs in the skis, sliding one leg forward and then another. When their turn arrived, they moved towards the loading deck but Lissy did not make it into place in time and Will was already up in the air in the chairlift. He swivelled himself around and called out to her to sit down as the chair arrived and pull the bar down over her head.

"That's it! You got it," he said. He was being an extraordinary big brother that day, not teasing her or making things more difficult.

And there she was on her way up the hill. She recalled the exhilaration as the chair lifted upward, high in the air. The ride was short and soon they were nearing the disembarkment platform. Will turned around and yelled out to her to lift the bar and then push herself off to the side. She managed to lift the bar but as the chair levelled with the top of the hill, young Lissy didn't move an inch, she was frozen to her seat. The chair continued on, around the terminal at the top of the hill. All eyes were on her.

"Mum? Mum!"

Lis, brought back to the present, looked at her son and saw panic shooting out towards her. She inhaled deeply.

"I'm okay," she said. "Just give me a moment."

They had stopped the lift for her at the bottom of the hill and the ski instructors had calmly helped her off to safety and into the arms of her mother, who had arrived on the scene just at that moment.

"Where's your brother? He's supposed to be helping you!"

One step at a time, she murmured to herself as she focused on the task at hand and slid herself along the rail by slowly lifting and moving her rear end and legs towards David. She was merely a metre away now. Lis heaved herself across the last leg and onto the safety of intact sleepers, where she lay face down, arms gripping the rail, the hard metal digging into her body, relieved to be safe. Lis hoped neither she nor David would remember these details later when they told their story sometime down the track. She could imagine the look of amusement on Sara's face.

Lis rose to her feet and, securing Chloe in the carrier on her back, they made their way along the tracks, no further dramas, until the tracks descended to ground level, the road just 10 metres beyond.

"Let's take a rest here," suggested Lis.

"Wagsy!" Chloe's tiny high-pitched voice called out excitedly. And there he was, panting and dusty but apparently no worse for wear.

Chloe's cute little voice played Lissy's heart like a wind instrument, conjuring up images of Sal, who at that age was chattering in her own language with a chirpy voice that made anyone within earshot smile. A flood of worries came crashing down. How was she going to find her daughter and keep her family safe? Gale and Sara floated into her mind like clouds casually meandering by. If she strained her attention she could almost hear them encouraging her to keep going, keep David and Chloe safe and head towards the Meeting Place, where hopefully she would meet up with her friends. Together they would figure out how to rescue Sal. It was a plan.

Lis pictured both Gale and Sara starring as superheroes in a thriller movie. Gale, although a rather serious and sombre sort, could be brilliantly strategic, with a reputation as an almost supernaturally gifted chess player, and was phenomenally successful in her career. Sara on the other hand, while certainly plagued by her ups and downs, was a big-picture thinker (and therefore a global doomsayer), a true empath, and intuitive to the point of paranormal ability to sometimes see into the future. Strangely Sara thought Lis to be a superhero herself.

"You have uncanny good luck," Sara told Lis one time while they sipped espresso martinis at the Levee Lounge. "You're able to squeak through against the odds. Not just win the lottery but survive those death-defying moments."

"I don't know," said Lis. "I think it's more that I'm a klutz; accidents want to happen around me."

"You just need to trust yourself," said Sara in a manner that made Lis pause, her chest opening as she put her shoulders back in an uncharacteristic manner.

The sound of a helicopter over to the north pulled David and Lis to their feet.

"How about that house on the hill?" Lis pointed across the road. Just next to the old cemetery by the road heading out of town was a lone house that would have been a chapel back in the day, now fully renovated with a new tile roof, no doubt replaced after the 2025 hailstorms besieged the area, and still showcasing stained-glass windows that caught Lissy's eye. As if on cue, Wags leapt to his feet and headed up the hill with Lis, David and Chloe in tow, moving quickly to avoid any further encounters.

Just as they crossed the road, Lis spotted the black beetle vehicles and figures just ten metres ahead at the intersection.

"Hurry, hurry," Lis urged David along as they quickly crossed the road and skirted the tree line to the house.

Not surprisingly, the door to the house was open. Lis was about to step in.

"Mum, we should make sure nobody else is here already," David cautioned.

"How did you get so smart!?" Lis exclaimed.

"All them zombie movies!"

"Those, not them, David."

"Yeh Mum, I know." David said with a cheeky grin.

Lis could see David straighten up his spine as he explained to her how they could throw a rock into the room up front, stay hidden and see what happened.

"First we do a recce around the house and peek into the windows without letting anybody see us!"

After checking the perimeter Lis and Chloe stayed hidden behind the Westringia bush that was still hanging in there through this never-ending drought.

Come to think of it, thought Lis, perhaps it was about to break. She thought she could see a few spots of grey in the otherwise clear sky.

David found a smallish rock and nominated himself as the most agile and likely one to succeed with this mission. Wags was to stay with Lis while David sidled his way to the house. As he brought his arm back to throw the rock, Wags leapt out and raced towards David and into the house to fetch the rock.

"Wags," David cried out.

He ran back to his mother and they crouched together as Wags returned merrily with the rock gingerly cradled in his frothy mouth. Lis and David waited for five minutes and, when there was no sign of life, no reaction from inside or outside the house, they gathered themselves up and moved through the front door and into the building.

Lis sighed and realised she had been holding her breath.

"We did it, we did it!" David was singing a victory song and wiggling his legs around in a happy dance. Wags trotted in circles around him and let out a few loud barks.

"Wags, shush," Lis quietened the dog but smiled at her son. David was beyond precious to her. He was clever, funny and imaginative in a way that could be very practical at times. They needed to find Sal. Soon. Very soon. It was already feeling too late, even though it had only been one day since the Round-up in her neighbourhood. She had no idea where Sal was. The only clue really was the black-helmeted guards stationed just around the bend. She made a mental note to put them at the top of her strategic ideas list for tomorrow. For now, she would settle David and Chloe. They all needed a feed and some rest after taking a good look around the house to make sure it was empty.

The lounge room sported an impressive rock fireplace that had caught Lissy's eye as they entered the house.

"My sword!" David called out gallantly as he grabbed the poker.

"Not that one David, too dangerous!" Lis insisted he surrender it to her and instead he chose the spade as his weapon.

Wags ran into the room with a lopsided gait, delighted with himself and his adventures. He had clearly been roaming the interior and found nothing alarming. Lis felt her fear level abate; it was good having a dog around at times. She settled Chloe on the sofa with Wags along with some Fruit Loops she found in the kitchen pantry, pleased to see that it was brimming with goods. Then, like a scene from a thriller, David and Lis made a show of it as they went from room to room of the single-storey house, David, the chivalrous knight in armour, pouncing into rooms and calling out while he waved the iron implement in circles to fend off any opponents.

Next stop, the kitchen, where Lis whipped up a Mexican-style meal with beans, rice, tacos and salsa. There was even a gas stove here and water came out of the faucet with good pressure as if nothing was wrong; the large tank outside must still be quite full. But, as they drifted off to sleep later that night, all of them in the one king-size bed, Lissy's thoughts were sombre, drenched in worry. She needed to find Sal. She needed to find her friends or anybody who could help her to find her daughter. Chloe was coughing again this evening and Lis and David were both fully exposed now to whatever Chloe might have been sick with. Her worries picked up momentum as the alarms once again took to the streets, the sound playing hauntingly through her sleep. The other three slept soundly while Lis tossed and turned, her nerves frayed and frazzled.

\*\*\*

Lis slipped out of bed at the crack of dawn. The drone of the sirens had ceased and it was a relief to hear herself think again. She opened the front door and looked around. From this vantage point on the small hill, there were no other houses near them except a couple of dwellings on the other side of the street, just past the railway tracks. Lis stepped outside and noticed the weather had taken a slight turn. For the first time in ages there were clouds in the sky, slightly palpable moisture hanging in the air. She turned her gaze towards the T-junction, where a perpendicular road headed to the industrial area and the main road continued out of town in the direction of Sara's place. Up the road beyond the T-junction, she spotted the square configuration of black vehicles. Lis couldn't see much more from where she was so she decided to get closer for further inspection.

She wasn't feeling particularly brave as she cautiously skirted the edge of the hedges and sparse tree line, keeping herself hidden and stopping when she was diagonally across from where the military-like installation was set up. She crouched low behind a good-sized bush and looked more closely at the two armoured vehicles, completely blackened, even the windshield glass, with headlights that protruded like the eyes of insects. She hoped that David and Chloe were still asleep back at home as she continued to observe the figure who now appeared from just up the street a bit behind the vehicles. He too was armoured head to toe, no clues offered as to his identity. For all she knew, these people could be an alien species descended to Earth for reasons she could not even fathom. A second figure appeared, pacing alongside the vehicles in almost mirror symmetry on the other side of the street. The quietness felt surreal, with no cars, no people, no aircraft, no activity at all other than the vehicles and guards. They would have to get past the roadblock either by heading into the low-lying shrubs around it or finding an alternative path.

Wags came racing up to Lis, belting out a fleeting bark that broke the stillness.

"Wags, shhhhh." But her shushing was unnecessary as the retriever fell instantly silent, his hackles bristling, and Lis held her breath for a moment waiting for the men to turn towards them. It was as if the guards were in a different dimension, oblivious to the dog's bark while they continued to patrol without losing a beat.

Lis decided it was enough of a reconnaissance for the moment and they returned to the house, where once again it was time for breakfast. For a little while Lis and her gang settled into the smell and crunch of maple syrup on waffles. They could not have landed in a better equipped kitchen; this one was laden with appliances, ample food and supplies, enough for months or perhaps even a year.

A full array of solar panels and batteries along with a large bottle of gas kept them in business. Even the refrigerator was running and still stocked up. Soggy greens and curdled milk needed tossing but yoghurt and butter were treasures ready to be lapped up as were the many condiments and a half dozen eggs, probably from the now vacant chook house out the back.

***

Chloe appeared to settle well into her new family in those first couple of days. She ran after Wags and chortled happily, amused even when she toppled over. Wags seemed happy to have them all around him in the house. Lis didn't dare let him out unattended for fear he would set alarms off and announce their arrival on the scene. With the four of them keeping their heads pulled in, the house became a playground for children, dog and sometimes Lis as well when for a moment she was able to distract herself from her heartache and worry about Sal … and about everything. The only rule she made was to keep the noise levels down, difficult to enforce with Wags and Chloe but Lis and David had taken to whispering much of the time, keeping their voices modulated while kicking a tennis ball around the house, aiming to score goals in the fireplace or through the kitchen door.

Somebody randomly looking in might have thought they were a thriving family, and in some ways they would be right, but much of the time Lis felt worried sick to her stomach, consumed by loss, overwhelmed. She tried to imagine what their next moves should be. Going back into town felt too risky with the alarms still sounding at night and she could see a new guard station just one block back, in the direction they had come from. They would need to get to Sara's place and find some help there or perhaps somewhere along the way.

In that first week, Lis slipped out once or twice a day, Wags often leading the way, to investigate how they might get past the guard station to continue their journey westward, out of town. She sought cover on the edge of the road behind the thick weeds, lone survivors that were barbed and scratchy and made it hard going. The days passed and Lis managed to get a bit further each time. After a week or so she finally made it to the next intersection only to be disappointed by a guard station positioned there as well. Dispirited, she returned home, mission aborted.

Now it was breakfast time once again at the Henderson's. Lis had seen their name on various papers around the house. Mandy Henderson had a kitchen "to-die-for", Lis mused. Rustic-modern with rose-granite benchtops, mauve patterned curtains and sleekly designed cupboards. Top that off with wide hardwood floorboards and a chunky picnic-style eating nook. Any other time she would have been blissed to be cooking here and, dreamer that she be, she did forget herself for moments at a time as she busied herself with more makeshift cuisine. Polenta pizza made from white corn meal, canned mushrooms and spaghetti sauce, tossed with grated parmesan cheese from a large white-specked block she discovered in the depths of the pantry. Once baked, David carved out stars, triangles and random zigzag shapes served on blue ceramic plates for the three of them. Actually, the four of them, as Wags also devoured this meal given there was no dog food on the premises. The retriever didn't mind in the least, voraciously gobbling up whatever was offered. No complaints there. A lone blue wren tapped steadily at its reflection in the windowpane, fending off a potential rival. This could have been an ordinary day in suburbia.

After lunch, they poured through an extensive collection of DVDs that accompanied a dusty player tucked away beneath the large smart screen TV. David and Chloe settled on the leather couch to watch a sci-fi comedy with Wags comfortably splayed on the woven antique rug next to the fireplace. Lis excused herself to slip out once more and see what was happening outside.

As she left the house her eyes took in the other-worldly orange haze in the sky and the unforgettable smell of forest fires met her nose, no longer any moisture in the air. Lis had lived through many fire seasons before but she had felt safe while living in town. Those who lived in the bush, like Sara, were more at risk. In the past, there would be firefighters on the ground and sometimes planes to dump water over the most urgently affected areas. None of that would happen now. She looked out and could spot the smoke to the south of town. They would need to get a move on.

Two more days passed and Lis breathed a sigh of relief that she and David had not caught whatever illness Chloe had before Lis discovered her in the supermarket. Time was punctuated by baked beans on white flour flatbreads, bowtie noodles with canned corn and tomatoes and, David's favourite, black bean tacos with brown rice. While David busied himself with inventing new knots and sharpening up tools he found in the cellar, Lis was preoccupied with finding Sal. Whatever ideas percolated in her mind they all boomeranged back to the need to find help, other survivors to band together with, others in search of their loved ones.

"How will we find Sal?" David enquired several times a day.

"We're going to get out of here soon and get some help," Lissy reassured him. "We'll find her and we can all go home."

Lis clung ferociously to this hope, never entertaining the possibility that Sal, her gorgeous, witty, stubborn daughter could be lost to her. She did not want to think about that any more than she had previously wanted to discuss the possible collapse of the world as they knew it. And yet here they were. Once more she concluded that they needed to make a move tomorrow morning. They would find a way to pass the guards and go find Sara or Gale. Or, for that matter, anyone else to share this awful crisis with.

# Part 3  Round-up Week 3

## July 2028

# 6    Sara

In the days following what I now refer to as the Round-up, I ventured down the road, the one drivable access point to the property, only to discover a roadblock and guards stationed there. I spent another day climbing the eastern ridge to Pyramid Scenic Road but it too was blocked where it meets the main road and I quickly turned back.

Since then I have been spending all my time on our block, a 20-hectare multiple occupancy that stretches from the road down to the creek by the forests that climb the ridges and forms the border between New South Wales and Queensland. I moved here in 2018 along with some friends, Zack and Tilly, Linda and Tom. Over the past few days I have become absorbed in digging up soil samples from around the property, looking for signs of life. During the spray regimes, paddocks were pummelled with toxic formulas meant to scourge the lands of rats and mice, especially in crop-yielding country, but unfortunately the spray stopped everything in its tracks, not just the plague of rodents. The soil became destitute, the billions of microorganisms that populate a teaspoon of soil destroyed instantaneously. Disastrous.

"Cataclysmic!" I jump, surprised at the sound of my own voice.

Having not had much success with the samples, I've decided to head to the Meeting Place again. Gale and I talked about a quarterly full-moon seasonal schedule to reconvene with Lis but I am keen to go there again just in case anyone has arrived. Pot was, of course, part of the plan too but everybody knows that my lovers come and go with the tides, so you never really know who the current one might be.

"I can't keep up!" my last foster mother used to say when I would give her a call now and then.

Thus far I have not met a soul at the Meeting Place or anywhere along the way.

I pack my bag with dried herbs, a variety of roots, taro and arrowroot, dried bananas and persimmons. Strangely the persimmon trees have survived the drought and the poisoning of the land and I was able to harvest, peel and sun-dry the fruit in the early autumn.

I glance about in all directions, ever wary of intruders, and search the skies for any flyovers. Everything looks, sounds and feels clear, so I snake my way down the old track to the creek. Or what used to be a creek. The vegetation is largely withered. Even lantana, once a robust and troublesome weed, is now reduced to mostly leggy brown sticks drooping haphazardly along the way.

I'm pleased at how well I blend into the languid landscape with my brown dyed T-shirt and muddied jeans, my skin resembling the sun-baked compacted earth. I guzzle water from a bottle to keep myself hydrated. This time there are no cane toads, or much movement at all, as the dry has really set in these past couple of weeks. In fact, there is very little here now. Dust. Dirt. Bones. The sun. The moon. Nary a cloud.

On the other side of the creek, I feel a tinge of excitement, a glimmer of hope. Here there are trees again, many of them still managing well, especially as the thinner sclerophyll forest gives way to rainforest. Last time I was at the Meeting Place, I thought I heard someone coming but it was a false alarm, wishful thinking perhaps. A small rodent or a skink scurrying by. The forest has suffered but it is still an oasis for the creatures. I wonder if they are aware that things have gone terribly off course or whether they have adapted to their new circumstances without any complaints.

I arrive at the spot, hang out for three days in anticipation and yet again it is another unsuccessful meet-up. No sign of Gale, Lissy or Pot. For that matter no sign of anyone. My heart sinks.

I return home.

I wake up feeling disheartened. A cat ambles by and I recognise it as the progeny of a long line of tall black cats with white socks that have frequented the land over the years. The cat will be killing the few small creatures that remain so I decide to leave food out for her that night. Keep her belly satisfied. She is the closest thing I have to company now, aside from the odd honeyeater and the blue wrens still hopping around on occasion where I have put out bowls of water and a seed mix I found up at Tilly's.

For the next few days, I laze around on what used to be the grass but is now hardened dirt with the odd weed, some couch grass and mostly the dreaded bindii that makes barefoot walking untenable. I sit and watch jumping ants at their nest in the dirt next to the cabin. I've always had a thing for ants. The highlight of my day is when I offer them honey on the end of a stick. One by one they come over and gather around the drop to sip the sweet nectar for their queen. They are organised and productive as always, rushing around, making nose to nose contact, trailing pheromones in their wake. I reckon you can count on the ants to be here with you at the end of the world. Yep, they are fine, the ants are fine; life goes on for them as always.

I can feel my mood continue to dip. I have been prone to periods of depression since my teens, and I've been on antidepressants for over a decade. My supply is about to run out so I have been halving the tablets to make them last longer but I am not sure if this is a good idea. I could be in for a bit of a rough ride.

I've lost all motivation for my soil project and attempts at growing food.

I wander about the land aimlessly. I pluck blue flower petals from the scotch thistle that is thriving in this dryness and munch on them. Some call it bushman's chewing gum as it adds some moisture to the mouth. Definitely an overstatement, but at least it's something.

At night I gaze at the evening stars, on the lookout for any constellations I can identify; anything familiar is comforting – the Southern Cross, the Big Dipper, Orion, and then there's always Venus to make a wish upon.

I wish an end to this frightening militaristic state.

# 7  Lis

"Mum, my throat is sore," David croaked early one morning. It had been two weeks since they'd arrived at the house on the corner. While Lis had meant to get a move on things, time had slipped away as she swirled in confusion about how to proceed. Lissy's stomach tightened. If David was infected with the H9 virus and possibly with Kawasaki or Reye's, there would be no help to be found. Sal missing, David sick. Hopefully Chloe had just had a regular cold or the flu. A few days and David would be better. Fingers crossed.

Lis hovered over David, worrying, fretting, ruminating, doing laps between the kitchen and the bedroom, bringing every remedy she could come up with working with the supplies that were on hand. David complained at the gargling, steaming and drinking concoctions with chilli and honey and who knew what else. Lis coaxed, insisted that he try, at least try, to swallow a few mouthfuls. By the second day, David was sneezing and coughing and feeling weak. Lis couldn't find a thermometer but a hand to the forehead was all that was needed to feel the heat emanating from her son's body. Soon he was shivering and sweating from where he lay below several blankets, despite the heat in the house.

It reminded her of that time she was in Bali in her early twenties. Gale and Sara had gone off to some tobacco-smoking, mushroom-munching, trauma-shaking thing with a guru while Lis had stayed back to enjoy a few slow days in Ubud. But when her stomach seized up and her head began pounding, she was unable to walk more than a few steps without becoming dizzy and spewing. She could feel the heat emanating from her chest and back, the sheets sopping wet with sweat. Lis pulled herself back into the present. She had lived through that episode (crawling to the door of her hotel room, laying collapsed in the hallway until someone found her) and David would get through this.

Lis kept up the regime of fluids and herbal remedies she discovered in the bathroom cabinet but, on the fourth day, David lay crying in bed. He had lost control of his bowels, not only embarrassing for him but also frightening for them both. Last year, he had lost his friend Rory, who lived a couple of blocks away, to the virus. Many young people had landed in ICU when the latest variation showed up before the Health Department put in place strict and absolute stay-at-home orders on all kids his age.

Lis was beside herself. David no longer wanted to eat, had lost his sense of taste and smell, and his mood darkened as he withdrew into himself. On the fifth day he refused a glass of water, pushing the glass out of his mother's hand, with it shattering on the floor.

"Leave me alone Mum," David moaned.

"We need to get you through this Davey. Please just try," she coaxed as she handed him some vitamin C pills she had found in the bathroom cabinet. David groaned and rolled over in the newly made bed, mounding pillows over his head and falling once again into a delirious sleep.

Lis ducked out to check if anything had changed outside but no such luck. The guards were still on duty around the bend so Lis returned to the house to feed Chloe and then continued to sit and fret by the bed. She hoped she wouldn't fall ill too or they would be in real trouble. H9 did not generally impact healthy adults that severely and she had been wearing a mask she found in the bathroom whenever she was near David. She didn't know much about Kawasaki and Reye's syndrome except she had seen images of children with swollen hands and feet, skin peeling and red eyes. At least for now David showed no such signs. But what if he developed swelling of the brain? She had heard something about that as well. Maybe that would explain his aggressive behaviour this morning. Her mind lurched out of control and she lay her head in her arms, hidden away for a few minutes.

Lis got herself back in motion and settled Chloe on some flat square cushions on the floor with various sized pots and containers to explore while Lis curled up in the green velvet armchair.

# Part 4 Round-up Week 5

## July 2028

# 8    Gale

The notches were accruing and a routine emerged, a familiarity, yet never a moment when she felt safe; the four walls of her cell threatened to obliterate her. As far as she could tell, aside from the weekly exercise in the corridor, she had been confined to the featureless concrete cube for five weeks now. The only movement in the cell was the small built-in portal where the food tray slid in and out, a bowl of mush. She had become accustomed to the food and convinced herself it was somewhat like the plant protein she used to buy in the supermarket. There was the weekly check-in from the voice but she had not been attended to or taken for medical treatment despite her plea for attention to her increasingly red and swollen wrist.

She spent hours striding back and forth in the confines of the cell under the insufficient ceiling vent, touching each wall as she paced. She sought a way to feel more spacious within the limited confines but the cell remained small, tight and dark. She worried she wouldn't have the wherewithal to survive this. Emmy was on the other side of the continent and Sara and Lis were who knows where. She might never see any of them again.

Gale and her friends had often discussed the unknown future. Impending collapse. Temperatures rising. Floods, droughts, fires, pandemics. And possible social mayhem. They had even spent time setting up the Meeting Place in case of complete chaos. But this was beyond what they had imagined. They hadn't prepared themselves for round-ups and imprisonment. She was trapped and alone, aside from the digital voice and presumably others in their cells adjacent to hers.

She had no idea what was wanted of her or what was in store for any of them. The senselessness struck her and she flung herself face down into the thin foam mattress. She remembered a chant from the rallies she had been to over the years, "The people united will never be defeated". But they were isolated here. No uniting. No movement. No secret underground. No communication at all. Solitary confinement. No victory glimmering faintly on the horizon.

At the following week's exercise period, Gale noticed that the heavier woman who had struggled to exercise was no longer there. In the sixth week, a couple of others were gone as well. What happened to them, where were they being taken to? She started to see a flowchart in her mind with an endless loop of meals on a tray and a light that blinked on and off. She could not find the exception to the rule. Yet. She would have to wait, try to stay calm enough to endure the walls around her. They closed in on her mind, squeezing the breath out of her chest, a pressure she was learning to at least tolerate. She had to.

The throbbing in her wrist increasingly worried her. She needed medical attention soon.

The next day, the voice greeted her once again.

"Good morning number 87."

"Hello, I need medical attention. My wrist is badly infected."

"How are you feeling today 87?" The voice asked the same question as always.

"Is there anybody there? I need medical attention!"

"Thank you. That will be all 87."

The voice echoed off the walls, unbothered by the heat of the cell.

She decided she would call out again when the food portal opened that evening in case somebody on the other side could help her. Like a tricky riddle, she pondered the precise words to reach out with during the few seconds the tray was incoming.

"Hello? Anybody there?"

Or perhaps, "I need a doctor."

She jerked backward at the sound of her voice in the room. She needed to think about this. There may be only one opportunity to get it right. Later that day, her plan failed, there was no reply and Gale heard not a peep from the other side of the portal.

She went to bed dispirited. Trapped in a state of purgatory that now cloaked her existence.

# 9  Lis

A scream pierced through Lissy's sleep. David bolted upright in the bed next to the camp cot that Lis had pulled into the room so she could be within arm's reach. With a groan he curled his small body into a protective shell, sheet thrown off his body to the side.

"David," Lis whispered and lay her hand on his forehead. It felt hot enough to fry an egg and moisture dripped down his back and neck.

"Try to get some sleep darling," Lis said softly.

David grunted and pulled the mangled sheet back up around his aching body.

"I'm cold," he said.

The house was quiet.

# 10  Sara

"Here kitty kitty."

I hate to admit it but I am pleased to see the tall black cat again, daintily prancing by the shack in the early hours of the morning. After no human contact for over a month, I am uplifted by this critter I now call Boots, even though I know they wreak havoc on native wildlife. I still see the odd wallaby about and the local goanna seems to be faring alright but a deep loneliness has sunk in. I talk to pretty much anything that moves – trees, snakes, insects. At least I'm not talking to the rocks yet, but who knows?

"Hello Rock," I say. I laugh.

In the first couple of weeks, I spent lots of time on garden projects. I tried to grow the soil, experimenting with ways to speed up the composting process. I had a bit of fun combining various fungi from the forest with comfrey and yarrow and any food scraps, along with plant matter and droppings from the odd bandicoot or wallaby that wandered by. Of course, there is an abundance of purslane, a succulent that loves to grow where nothing else can, it loves dry hard dirt and even grows on pavement! Tastes like asparagus when steamed, quite yummy. That said, food growing has been painstakingly slow but fortunately I still have a healthy stash of dried legumes, grains and pasta, though I have been eating my way through them. There's even more at Zack and Tilly's place, and then again at Linda's shack and Tom's house just a bit further up the property. I'm certainly not suffering from malnutrition. In fact, the other day I could feel my favourite holey jeans tightening around my waist. Most days I just wear trackies now or cut-off shorts, T-shirts or singlets or even nothing on the extremely hot days. There's nobody to see me and, although for a while I half expected to see our neighbour Fi trotting along on her horse from over the other side of the national park, there have been no humans on the property or along the road.

Unfortunately, my mental health has been slaloming downhill of late, leaving in its wake a heaviness that puts pressure on my chest, pervades my whole body. It doesn't help that my thoughts are spinning tirelessly in circles. What is happening? Why is it happening? Where does it extend to? Worrying, worrying. There is uncertainty in all directions regardless of my attempt to make sense of things. Equally troublesome for me is how I will manage my mental health. I absolutely dread depression, having battled with it off and on in my earlier years and now I no longer have any medication left. I'll need to find a way to ride this out. Somehow.

I spend much of this week lying on the couch eating bowls of popcorn cooked up on the wood stove and dressed with oil, chilli flakes, garlic and salt, while binge-watching movies I've stashed on my old portable hard drive that I dig up from a box below my bed. I almost enjoy myself as I compulsively munch my way through a series of zombie end-of-the-world films followed by every single episode of *Twilight Zone*, an old black and white American sci-fi horror series, before I move onto a selection of Australian films made in the Northern Territory. I bawl my eyes out through *Rabbit Proof Fence*. As a child who was taken away into foster care at a young age and still does not know her biological family, I often wonder who my mob is, where I am from. I find the films provocative and I imagine hopefully that there could be pockets of people living in remote communities who have escaped the round-ups and are managing to survive the debilitating dehydration of the intense desert heat. Maybe the round-ups are localised to the Northern Rivers or the whole of New South Wales. I really have no idea what is happening in the rest of the country or even the world.

I could pack it up, venture out and see what I find, but I don't want to abandon ship just yet. Gale and Lis are both very resourceful and I can wait another two seasons for their return. And Pot of course. I have this horrible sinking feeling in my gut that I will never see Pot again. I can well imagine them putting up a fight and then being taken down. Gale, on the other hand, is practical, strong and smart as a whip; if anyone can survive it will be her. I do expect to see her again. Lis is, of course, none of those things. I smile as I think of her, a romantic dreamer, a free spirit. She is lucky as well. I remember that time she almost drove her car over a cliff, Sal in the baby seat in the back, the grey Subaru perched precariously on the edge. Somehow Lis managed to slip out with Sal, no problem, completely unscathed and very matter of fact about it afterwards. I shake my head and a small giggle escapes as I think of Lissy's quirky ways. She's a good stick.

After I emerge from my musings, I dash out to the kitchen to cook up the first of a series of pasta dishes made with shiitake mushrooms that I dried out last year. Then I return to the couch once again, with the steaming dish and a local craft beer I am pleased to have found at Tom's place. Over the next couple of days, I feast as I work my way through the *Matrix* movies, *Men in Black* and then the original *Star Trek* series. By the end of *Discovery*, I have taken to eating peanut butter from the jar for breakfast and have brewed up some coffee I found at Linda's, along with condensed milk that I found hidden at the back of her pantry. Beyond delicious.

Everything is a jumble. I have started to lose track of time. It has polarised into "before the Round-up" – a steady decline of ongoing drought, fires and pandemics – and "after the Round-up", this aimless life on the land. I can feel my days whirling down a basin like the flush of a toilet. A bottomless eddy that sucks away at both the land and the people. I'm having trouble thinking straight. Even my diary entries are a bit jumbled of late, mostly letters to Gale thinking back to the good times we had and wondering if we will ever be reunited.

I continue to seek solace in the night sky, sending my prayers out to the dancing galaxies, but nothing changes.

# 11    Gale

The monotony was torturous. Gale continued to exercise in
her cell, eat meals and devise ways to keep herself occupied,
such as multiplying two-digit numbers in her mind – first
12 x 12 through to 19 x 19 and then mixing them up –
16 x 14, 15 x 17 – and when she was up for it, 67 x 23 or
78 x 92 and so on. She had always had a nimble mind and
enjoyed putting it to a calisthenic test. Gale tried to picture
a chess board to make up a series of moves. This task,
however, was beyond her grasp and she looked for a way to
make something that would do the job here in her cell. When
the next meal came, Gale took pieces of the stodgy food
and sacrificed the meal to make board pieces: small balls
for the pawns, thin, tall pieces for king and queen and more
squat pieces with small variations for the rooks, bishops and
knights. Not a fabulous set but over the course of a few days
the pieces hardened and she managed to get a workable game
happening using the brown drink to make the lines of a board
in the corner of her cell on the floor.

Gale imagined she was playing against those who
were behind this round-up. Perhaps it was the Department
of Public Health, which had taken extreme measures with
the spray regimes, and yet she had the sense that it could
just as easily be a right-wing faction that had overtaken the
government or even a foreign-led coup. The political scene
had become increasingly unpredictable and ludicrous ever
since the Trump-inspired riots on the US Capitol in 2021
followed by his decisive victory in the 2024 election. Media

was increasingly unreliable as it became next to impossible to know what was real news and what was fake, deepfake images and videos increasingly doctored or fully fabricated by AI, news simply one person's version of reality versus another's. Impossible to even know at this point who was really in power and who would have initiated this sequence of extreme events.

Gale set up scenarios on her board to play out different openings: Sicilian, Queen's Gambit, French, Scandinavian, until she tired herself out once again. Stalemate. Very difficult to beat an opponent who would not show their face.

# 12  Lis

Lis was gazing at David's body curled up tightly on the bed.
He had barely eaten a morsel in several days and when he
did manage to take a few mouthfuls, he was unable to keep it
down. Anxiety gnawed hungrily at Lis as she worried that he
would develop further complications from the virus. At the
best of times, David was small and wiry, prone to stomach
aches and nosebleeds. He had been born with a condition
called gastroschisis, with his abdomen and the top part of his
intestines protruding outside his body. It had been a medical
miracle that he had grown into a healthy, bright and vibrant
young person who used his small size to his advantage,
swinging from the ropes in the gymnasium and taking to the
rock-climbing wall with gusto.

   With no internet to scour, Lis recited a litany of
disease names to herself, counting them off as if on a ticker
tape: meningitis, encephalitis, Reye's syndrome, Kawasaki,
tuberculosis. She could not remember which of these was
deadly, which required antibiotics. In any case, there were
barely any pills to choose from in the bathroom cabinet
located above the sink. She shuddered at the thought of
venturing out into the neighbourhood in search of antibiotics.
A small tubule with Chinese characters scrolling vertically
caught her eye. Miniscule sideways writing indicated they
were for colds and flus. Lis gave the small bead-like black
pills a sniff. Her acupuncturist had once given her something
just like that and she decided to give them a go. David
managed to swallow them with water and a small groan. He

had weakened to the point that he no longer protested when she brought him her latest remedies. But they were out of everything now. No more garlic, ginger or chillies. No more pain killers, cough medicine or tissues to blow his nose with. Lis curled up in the armchair while she brushed Chloe's hair, Wags at her feet. She whispered a story about a silly wombat and a sneaky echidna to the little girl, more to keep herself calm than anything else.

# 13  Sara

Boots must think I've really lost it. Maybe I have. I'm shaking like a rag doll, bouncing my body up and down, my low hanging boobs making slapping sounds against my belly. Animals in the wild do this shaking action to release trauma. I think it works for us too. Flashbacks I would rather not remember pop up in my mind, but that's the idea. For a minute I freefall to the past and see myself pressed down on a bed, the up-and-down motion blends with the memory of a body on top of me. I was helpless. Much too young. He was too big and strong and scary. I focus my eyes back on the Bangalow palm and the callistemon to my right, two strong survivors. I can learn from them, their steadiness and adaptability. I feel my jaw loosening as I bop up and down, feet planted firmly on the cracked soil. But there is no relief. Images from the past bombard me like a photo album opened fanlike in my mind. I allow the visuals to arise and then change them, shift them to black and white, decrease their size. That's the practice I have learned and, when possible, I imagine Ninja-Sa, the magnificent warrior woman in her full glory. She enters the scene and spectacularly rescues the little girl, me, after removing the violators.

"Ninja-Sa to the rescue!" I call out.

"Ninja-Sa here I come!"

I am yelling now, no longer thinking about whether I am jeopardising my safety as I bounce bounce bounce, releasing, crying out, until finally I collapse in a heap on the ground, exhausted.

An hour later it is all a blur but I notice my heart is a little less heavy, my mind a bit less confused. Boots is now lying on my verandah next to the dish of dog food I put out for her. Zak used to have a dog and I found half a dozen tins of food in his pantry. Lucky Boots.

# 14  Gale

Gale was sitting slumped in her cell, staring, eyes glazed, at her food on the cold metal table, the very same blandness once again. It had been almost two months now in solitary confinement, no contact with anybody other than seeing the remaining women in the hallway during the wordless weekly exercise routine. The walls were concrete, solid, soundless. Her mind was blank, as if sedated. Gale put another spoonful in her mouth absentmindedly. She wondered about the woman on the other side of the wall, whether she was still there after the incident during yesterday's exercise period. The young dark-skinned woman had abruptly broken stride and turned around. Gale could see a wildness in her eyes as they darted this way and that. With a cry, the woman beelined to the exit doorway and promptly slumped to the floor with a moan. She was still there at the end of the session. Gale wondered if she had disappeared like many of the others or whether she was back in her cell now. She could almost sense her pacing back and forth like Gale herself often did, a lion enclosed with no way out.

Gale shovelled another spoonful of slop into her mouth, eyes turned downwards towards the plastic tray. It occurred to her to pick the tray up and thump it against the wall. Lazily she lifted the tray. *Thump, thump.* The muted tone reverberated in her cell but she doubted it could be heard through the thick walls. *Thump, thump.* And again. It felt liberating to hit the wall and she gave it a few more good whacks. The tritones would ring through the speaker any moment now to announce the end of breakfast. She would return her tray through the portal or there would be no dinner that evening. Deflated, she sat down and shovelled the last spoonful into her mouth, unaware she was chewing. Her eyes were blank, empty of life. The portal slid open. Gale pulled herself to her feet to return the tray. She paused after the first step. She could hear three muffled thuds drumming back through the wall. The portal slid shut and silence resumed. For a moment, Gale's eyes lit up. She imagined the woman next door, no longer pacing.

# 15 Lis

Lis passed much of her days keeping a worried eye on David while playing with Chloe, who liked to toddle around and hide behind furniture in a game of peek-a-boo, interspersed with chasing Wags, as she fully enjoyed the lopsided movement of her body as it teetered around the house. The two of them even snuck out to the backyard now and then for a few breaths of air and a feel of the ground beneath their feet while Wags attended to his business.

It was clear that David was not on the mend. The little black pills and all her remedies and concoctions had not done the job. While many of David's initial symptoms had passed, now he had a wracking cough that shook his whole body as he spat up phlegm and mucus. Lis knew a thing or two about illness. It seemed her mother had been sick with everything under the sun in the last decade before her untimely death at age 64. Lis had always thought there was something not quite right about her mother. Sometimes she held a blank look on her face as if she had broken away from this plane of reality. Not just daydreaming like Lissy, but detached, vacant. Nobody home. You could practically wave a hand in front of her face and she would not blink. Lis recalled that at one point her mother had shingles, a virus that then gave way to pneumonia, a bacterial infection. She postulated that this was what was happening with David. He needed antibiotics, now. She would need to venture out into the neighbourhood and hopefully a nearby house had some in their medicine cabinet. Or else she would have to head to the South Lismore chemist but there could be several guard stations between here and there.

Lis brought David some water and plumped up his pillows, then let him know she was going out in search of medicine. She would take Chloe with her, she decided, but at the last minute she brought Chloe back, safer in these circumstances inside the house.

"You stay here with David and Wags," she told Chloe as she brought her some rice crackers she had found and a set of children's blocks that had been boxed up in the closet of one of the bedrooms.

"Wagsy?" Chloe asked.

"Yes, Wagsy will stay here. You play with him and these toys. I am going to shut the door and I will be back very soon."

Lis hoped this was true. Chloe's mother had not come back – neither had Lis's daughter – and she had seen nobody on the road outside for weeks. Lis wondered for a moment where all the people had been taken to. Maybe the correctional facilities or quarantine buildings, or perhaps somewhere like the Nauru or Villawood refugee detention centres. A shiver travelled up her spine.

"I'll be back soon," she called out as she closed the door.

# 16  Sara

I wrote this letter in my diary this morning.

Dear Gale

These past few days I have been sitting on my verandah for hours at a time without moving. Like a surreal brass sculpture of a post round-up catatonic woman who unfortunately did not have her wits about her to survive. Once again, I seem to have collapsed in a heap and my movements have been confined to that red squiggle chair that reminded you of lollipops, interspersed with horizontal lie-downs in bed.

I remember that time in college, the look on your face when you burst into my room after I stopped responding to your calls. There was a fleeting moment of shock, perhaps even pity, that registered fleetingly on your face and was then superseded by Gale the Efficient – Gale, the one who takes charge and always knows what to do in every difficult situation. And just like that, the blinds were pulled open, fresh air came gushing into the room, clothing was quickly plucked off the floor, dirty food and plates were swept up and carted off to the kitchen.

Then the warmth and an uncharacteristic caring in your blue-grey eyes as you sat by me, by my side on the bed, a slight look – I think I would call it a twinkle – in your eye that let me know we would laugh about this moment later in our lives when it would seem like a mere drop of water in the bucket of time. Seeing you like that, I couldn't resist at least trying for a moment. It was as if you came into my dorm room, grabbed my marooned ship and dragged it out of the mire, pointed it in the right direction and then blew on it from behind, infusing it with the energy needed to continue its journey through rocky seas.

It kills me that I am not there for you now, wherever you may be, perhaps stranded as well, and instead I am here wallowing in self-pity, here on the land, torn between staying here or risking my safety to venture out beyond our Meeting Place. As planned, I'll wait two more seasons in hopes that you and Lis manage to get here.

Love Sa

*\*\**

My music is mournful, stirring, violins and a sweet melody filled with sorrow, only the mildest hint of anything resembling hope. I have spent several days now sitting silently, immobile on the rotting wooden verandah, barely moving to even swat a march fly or to have a sip of water. After I write another letter to Gale, it tickles the part of me that yearns to reach for wellness, to at least make the effort to get healthy enough to think clearly, make a plan and somehow make things right in a world gone horribly awry. The sun has been shining brilliantly for days, the temperature hovering around 40 degrees most of the time and my solar system is still pumping as well as my music collection. Good that I had the forethought to download a heap of tunes before the end of the internet. I put my headphones on, not wanting my music to waft out over the valley. I am mustering the energy to go raid Zack and Tilly's cupboard and cook up something healthy to eat. That's the plan, but instead I end up in a heap on the floor once again, weeping for hours on end, strains of electronic Bach sending me into waves of sadness so deep that I fear I am falling, falling, into a black hole from which I might never emerge.

I feel broken, my heart is shattered. Here I am in a situation that I have anticipated much of my life. I've even relished the thought of the collapse, seeing the potential of everything being revamped and transformed to more sane and caring ways of living. Yet clearly I don't have the resources. I can't find the courage to face it squarely and do something constructive, to at least help someone out there, if not Lis, Gale and Pot, to be able to even help myself. Without my antidepressants and my friends, I'm nothing. It's as if everything is turning to dust and so is my soul. I am losing integration, scattering like a handful of barren dirt tossed into the winds. I slip back into reverie.

"Wake up Sara."

"I don't want to."

"Look, there's Gale, just outside."

I squint my eyes.

"I don't see her."

"Look again."

"Gale?" I ask the shadow beyond. "You look different."

"Nothing stays the same, Sassy," Gale replies.

I had forgotten that Gale used to call me that. And I used to call her Guy and tease her about being such a boy, always sensible, more one for doing than talking, a bit of a tough nut to crack, and persistent, painfully persistent.

"We're in a real pickle now Guy," I say. "Remember that time we were lost in the bush and I was trying to lead us out, being the bush gal and all?"

"Bush gal!" Gale echoes.

"But I kept bringing us back to the same hollow strangler fig."

"The one we stood in together," whispers Gale.

"Very close," I say. You had this wry smile on your face the whole time, as if an inside joke was playing.

"Are you done?" you finally asked. "Shall I take us out now?" And then magically Guy, you led us 100 metres this way, 50 metres that way, as if you had a map in your head. You remember?"

There is no response and I see now that I am looking at a small pademelon, a rare sight these days. How does it still manage to stay alive? Gale, or Guy as I fondly call her, is no longer here and I am struck by an aching loneliness that spreads through my chest. I curl up in the bed, praying to fall asleep, into the void. "Guy," I whisper.

\*\*\*

Time continues to pass even in the haunting stillness of the land. Okay, c'mon Sara, I think as I notice the onslaught of self-doubt and recrimination. Enough of this wallowing. I need to get up, get some food in me, take a shower, hike out to the guard post to see what's happening there and in the valley. Time to get this show on the road.

I gather myself up; that is how it feels. At first, like lugging a sack of lead but, as I put one foot in front of the other, I can feel my mood lift ever so slightly and my pace quickens. Soon I am in Tilly's kitchen, where I decide to cook up some Japanese taro I harvested along the way with some canned peas I found in the pantry. Miraculously there are still a few sprigs of mint near the water tank. I make myself at home using their cooker, still connected to an almost-full gas bottle, and soon I am eating the first tasty meal I have made in a few days: taro, peas, olive oil mixed with cumin seeds, mint and garlic that Zach and I harvested from our shared garden last spring.

It is late afternoon and the wind picks up, sending dust and pollen blustering. I am surprised to see a cloud or two cloak the sky over the ridge, breaking the long stretch of hazy muted skies, as parched for moisture as the land below. With a good feed in my belly, I slowly let out a deliberate sigh as I imagine the potential rainfall that could fill the water tanks and drench the land, maybe even bring the creek to life once again. Tomorrow morning I should clean the gutters.

The sight of several fairy-wrens twittering in a clump of weeds, along with the possibility of rain, lifts my spirits and I decide to head down the road and check on the guard post. Turning right out of the driveway, I set off at a brisk pace along the road. Our house is the last one of six on the dirt road before it meets up with the main road to town. I haven't been to any of the other houses since just after the Round-up, when I found them all vacant and filled with supplies that I might need one day. I go down Lil and Ted's drive and then Cat's. They look untouched since I was last here, very little overgrowth as well, since not much can grow these days. Another 40 metres or so down the road I turn into Paul's place. Paul is, or perhaps I should say "was", a man in his sixties who kept to himself, with a penchant for fixing things up, making old machinery into new objects to make his off-grid living easier. The yard is littered with rusted-out cars and white goods as well as half-finished contraptions. There's a makeshift conveyor belt that stretches from the house to the shed, with a wheeled cart on it and a bicycle-like machine with a bowl, perhaps a grinder for dehulling grains. Lots of assembled unidentifiable metal trinkets that could have been artworks if nothing else.

I'm interrupted in my scanning by the gravelly sounds of men's voices floating over from inside the house. I quickly hide myself behind the shed wall as I spot movement along the side verandah, where I can make out the face of a thirtyish man with a long, pointed beard, his right arm by his side dragging a rifle casually like you would a rag doll. He sits himself down on an old faded armchair after grabbing a can of VB from a small bar fridge just within reach.

"Hey bud, did I tell you I saw that feral cat wander by yesterday?" he calls into the house. "Let's fatten it up, make us a gud feed. I'm getting tired of the roo we ben eatin'. Goanna up the road at that brick-and-mortar place mind you. Wanna head up there, see if we can score that for dinner?"

I can't make out the reply from inside the house but I have heard enough and I slowly slink away along the side of the drive until I reach the road again. Panicked, I turn on my heels towards home, instantly imagining the worst of these men, my mind spinning in all directions at once.

I arrive back home in a rush. Suddenly I am thrust to the end of what has been a largely unproductive but non-threatening day-to-day existence. I have struggled with my inner demons, putting all my energy towards staying strong enough for six more months in the hope of meeting up with Gale and Lis. Now everything has changed. Although I did not hear much, my sense is that these men are not kindred spirits or anything close to that. As I picture that man's face in my mind and hear those voices, I imagine the mean bony hillbilly type of men from that 1970s classic flick *Deliverance*. My step quickens and I know I will have to leave home immediately. If I could get past the many guard stations, I could go to Lissy's house in town but that feels all too dangerous.

I decide to head to the Meeting Place and hunker down there until I find a way to get out of the valley. My thoughts are interrupted. I feel a strange presence as if I am looking into Gale's eyes as she advises me to slow down and take stock of what to bring. As much food as possible, of course, although there is plenty up there and loads of water. I pause and can feel her prodding me to think through a bit further. "Medical supplies!" I exclaim aloud. The full kit. I make a note to get this together later. Already we have a small first aid kit at the Meeting Place along with a cooker, utensils and blankets. Maybe some extra clothing and, okay, a few books for Gale. I cannot let go of the thought that she is going to meet me there, and hopefully Lis too. I have given up on Pot. They have not shown up all these days that I have been here on the land and I am not hopeful. I urge myself forward on my mission to get as many supplies as possible up to the Meeting Place for future use, as I worry that down here is becoming unsafe and could become even more so.

Back at the shack, I pull out my large backpack from under the bed and decide to raid the food cupboards at Zack and Tilly's, Linda's and Tom's, after I set up a place to stash the supplies nearby. Not too close in case those men come looking but close enough to stock it up temporarily and then cart it over the next few days up to the Meeting Place.

A hundred metres down the track, I duck into the bush and lay out a few tarps. As I do so I realise that the ground is so dry there is probably no need. It's not likely to rain in the next few days, although in the late afternoon a slight cloud coverage in the sky teases once again and the temperature feels as if it has dropped a good 10 degrees. On my way back to Zack's, I check the thermometer at my place and sure enough it is now 30 degrees at 5 p.m. It being winter, the days are short and I am not sure how well I will sleep tonight knowing those men are just down the road. Sounds like they will be heading to Darren's place in any case; his is the sturdiest house on the street, bricks, concrete and a steel foundation.

I sling my big red backpack over my shoulders and head up to Tom's place first, grab his wheelbarrow, roll it right into his kitchen and proceed to load everything I can from the pantry to the barrow. Then I roll down the hill past my place and over to the temporary holding nook, unload and repeat this process. I work this way until 6 p.m. when darkness blankets the valley, having already raided Linda's place and then Zack and Tilly's. This has all led to a very impressive heap of cans and sacks and white buckets filled with legumes and grains. Everybody living around here has been quite proactive over the past few years, stocking up on goods in case another pandemic rolls in or cyclones and floods or other extreme weather events. Each person has had their own thoughts and predictions about all this. Unfortunately, mine have been the ones that seem to have played out. Military control along with disastrous climate conditions where food growing is next to impossible.

When I finally lie down to sleep after lots of lugging about, I realise that the urgency and busyness of the effort has taken me away from my usual overwhelm of feelings and moodiness. As a matter of fact, I haven't felt this well in months. Purposeful movement puts the limbo state at a standstill for a moment. I will cook up a plan tomorrow to get the goods moved to the Meeting Place, along with any other essentials from my place. I might as well take as much as possible as I no longer feel safe here. Not that I ever was, but the guards have never ventured out this way and in truth it has been strangely quiet these past couple of months. Since the round-up there hasn't been a single threatening event. Other than my internal lapses in mental health. Who would have thought that the real threat lies within me?

# Part 5 Round-up Week 9

## August 2028

# 17 Gale

It was another day. Breakfast arrived as usual, yet everything felt different. While they had their trays, there was contact with her neighbour. Thumps on the wall. What to do with that? Gale paced her cell, immersed in thought. The glow from the yellow overhead light kept her company, casting her shadow in front when she walked away from the light, behind her when she walked towards it. The woman on the other side of the wall might be doing the same. Thinking, pacing. Futility edged between Gale and her shadow and threw her down on the mattress with a moan of despair. A thud through a wall was in no way an escape plan. Even if they could develop a code to communicate, it would take forever and the woman next door was just as trapped as she was. They were bound to be seen banging on their walls by the eye in the ceiling, and who knew the consequences? The reason for their incarceration was obscure to say the least, as were the consequences of any wrongdoing. With a shaky sigh, Gale pulled herself up and commenced the day's 100 prisoner squats, an aptly named exercise. The only thing she could think to do for now was to stay fit. She felt dull, dispirited, and continued mechanically, safe in the familiarity of the movement, graceful in her precise execution.

Much later, as far as she could tell, perhaps the middle of the night, she roused from sleep. She guessed she had been asleep for several hours but the heat in the cell was making her extremely restless. She was crawling out of her skin. It was hotter than usual. The pain in her wrist was hot and burning as well. It was dead quiet. She couldn't recall if there had been a background hum previously from the slight ventilation coming from the ceiling, but certainly nothing now. She slipped back into a disturbed sleep that was riddled with nightmares and she did not wake up fully until the tones rang and the portal opened once again.

The tray was there as usual. And the bowl. And the spoon. And the cup. But no food. Nothing to eat and she could see that the bowl was still dirty from the last meal. Gale grabbed the tray and thumped on the wall repeatedly. She could hear the response from the next cell almost instantaneously. A rhythmic exchange began. Meaningless and yet meaningful in all that it delivered: connection, contact, another human.

The tones sounded and Gale slid the tray back into the portal. She hoped meals would resume at dinnertime. Maybe there was some kind of temporary glitch. Come to think of it, she had not heard from the voice for over a week now. She passed some more time doing a few lunges and her usual side-to-side pacing, leaning down to touch the walls. Sweat dripped down her temples, the saltiness a welcome taste upon her tongue. She thought of Patches, her tabby, licking her sweat with his gritty tongue. She missed him. At least he wouldn't be lying in his bed waiting for her to come home and feed him. Several months ago he had been crushed under the wheel of a speeding car. Gale wondered how she was going to die, how this was all going to end.

Another couple of foodless days passed. Twice a day the portal opened and the tray with dirty bowl, cup and spoon sat taunting, evidence that there had once been a feeding routine. From the moment she awoke, she felt a dreadful weight descend on her chest as if a 10-kilo dumbbell lay atop her. Her belly gnawed constantly, sinking Gale to the bottom of her emotional reservoir. She tended to be able to think her way out of difficult situations but she was overwhelmed with the discomfort in her body. Heavy, tight sensations in her chest rivalled the throbbing in her wrist, now quite visibly red and swollen. Alone in the hollow darkness, she and her neighbour tapped back and forth during the times when the portal door was open. Gale continued to return her tray in case meals were to resume. Some small reassurance to know there was someone alive, next door, in the same predicament as her. The heat, the throbbing and hunger melded into a state of numbness that left Gale sitting with her back against the wall for long stretches of time. She moved from there to her mattress where she lay in a foetal position. She could die like that, she thought. She felt weak, hot and tired. She had no idea what to do. Stress and anxiety were long-term bedfellows for her; she knew how to breathe, relax, tap, listen to guided visualisations, an overabundance of techniques to manage those sorts of issues. Now she lay in a heap. There was nothing else to do.

# 18  Lis

Lis turned down Terania Street just in time to see a bony-looking cow cross the street and amble over to a house, where it chewed nonchalantly on some weeds in the front garden. Other than that, it was deadly quiet. Not a sound coming from the guard station up the road. Lis quickly turned into a side street where she hoped to move around safely. As she approached the first house on the left, she saw what looked to be a figure sitting in a rocking chair on the concrete slab in front of the house. She stopped and had a better look. An old woman knitting? Lis couldn't believe her eyes. All this time she had assumed nobody else had escaped the Round-up, at least no sign of anybody anywhere near where she was, and here was a person casually rocking away, seemingly relaxing.

"Hello?" she called out.

The woman raised her eyes to Lis, knitting needles stopping mid-air.

The woman nodded at her but made no move to get up.

Lis approached, cautiously.

"I … I didn't know anybody else was still here," she said, calling out from the edge of the property where she stood on the footpath.

"Ah …" the woman replied. Lis could see now that she was in a well-worn nightgown, old beaten-up slippers on her feet.

"I'm looking for antibiotics for my son. He's very sick," Lis said.

The woman waved the needle in her right hand towards town and, as if to end the conversation, put her head down and continued her knitting.

"None here then? Anybody else around?" Lis asked in a voice that sounded more like Chloe's.

She wasn't sure but she thought the older woman shook her head imperceptibly.

Lis turned back and rounded the corner at Terania Street. She was about to head further into town when she caught sight of two guards standing under the railway overpass just ahead. She thought she heard someone cry out and she suddenly panicked at the thought of David and Chloe home alone. She quickly turned back towards the house, relieved as she entered and closed the door behind her.

Mission aborted.

# 19  Sara

Overnight the clouds continued to roll in and this morning a few drops manage to make their way optimistically down. I briefly wonder if a hailstorm might arrive, judging from the intense heat and the smudges of clouds tantalising over the ridge.

There are two ways to the Meeting Place once you get down to the creek. The most direct way is to head up the creek and then cut through the bush. In the past this was a rock-hopping adventure, the cool water swirling and dancing its way downstream, but nowadays it is mostly dry bedrock, easy to navigate. Alternatively, you can duck through Keith's property on the opposite side of the creek, wind through a stand of gum trees on a track that reaches the ridge road that cuts through the national park, then head north-east for ten minutes or so and drop down easily to the Meeting Place. I make the choice to head this second way today because it will be much easier with a heavy backpack weighing me down. I am tempted to try to get the wheelbarrow through as well but, with the food in it, it is far too heavy and it would be gruelling to move it on the track so I leave it behind. I may even run into Gale or Lis along the road. I know, very wishful thinking. I have been called naive once or twice in my life.

I am plodding along the ridge road when the sound of gunshot startles me out of my reverie. It sounds like it is further up the road so I cautiously press forward until I reach the site of a minor landslip that, after the 2022 floods, rendered the road impassable to cars and was never repaired.

I pause for a moment and decide that, to be safe, I will cut down through the bush even though the usual way down is just up ahead. Suddenly a smallish rock scuds to a halt right before my feet along the paved road. An accurate throw, if it was intended, that immediately gets my attention. I look up and see a figure moving towards me. He looks young and lifts his hand in salutation, as if to say hello. I take my backpack off and hide it in the bush in case I need to retreat quickly and begin to edge my way closer. As we near each other, I see an adolescent boy, perhaps fifteen or sixteen years old, with startling shoulder-length wavy blond hair and milky white skin. Strangely he is wearing a blue pin-striped collared shirt tucked into a pair of jeans with leather belt and a good solid pair of work boots on his feet. We continue to approach each other until our eyes meet. I am blown away by the dazzling intensity of his azure eyes, the first human eyes I have peered into in months. This encounter feels unusual and a jolt of energy zaps through my body. The boy, who on closer examination is perhaps more of a young man, looks at me with what seems to be recognition, as if he is expecting me and he casually but firmly gestures to me to come with him up the road. I hesitate as this is the direction the gunshot came from. The young man directs his eyes towards mine again and motions towards where we must go. I signal back that I will be a moment and fetch my backpack, then follow him as we move quickly up the road. In silence.

I am alert as we round the bend and my attention goes towards a form just up ahead lying sprawled on the road, not moving. It is a woman and I move closer, still alert to my surroundings, and then closer yet again. Seeing her reminds me of a wallaby I hit with my car one time. Shivering, trembling, bleeding ... and after a few minutes it gathered itself together, breathing heavily, and leapt into the bush magnificently. This woman though, most likely the boy's mother, has clearly been shot between her shoulder and her heart. She is barely conscious, moaning softly. I am now Sara-in-wilderness-rescue mode. Yep, this is my sort of thing. I rise to these emergency situations, then, as you well know by now, I fall apart later.

I examine the woman more closely and can see that her pectoral muscle has been torn open. I will need a medical kit. My good one is still down at the shack sitting by the door ready to go but there are quite a lot of supplies at the meet-up point, which is maybe 30 metres down the ridge from where we are standing. I am worried that whoever has the gun could be returning at any moment.

"We should move her off the road," I say.

The young man nods his agreement.

"Whoever did this could be back any minute now."

He shakes his head.

"They won't be back here?"

He shakes his head once more. Knowingly. Our eyes meet again and I can sense that he somehow knows this.

"There is a place just down there." I point.

He nods his head with understanding.

"There are medical supplies, food, water. Let's move her off the road into the safety of the bush where we can have a closer look, see if we can stop the bleeding."

Now that I look more closely, I see that both mother and son are thin as a rail, their facial bones accentuated, clearly not stuffing their faces as I have been these past few months. It cannot be easy for anyone during these times and who knows how these two have kept themselves alive. I think back to my wilderness first aid training and how to make a quick stretcher but there is no time. We pick her up together. I hold her back and shoulders, head resting against me while the young man takes her calves and feet into his arms. We make our way into the bush but it is slow going as I have my backpack on as well and we move cautiously for about 20 metres among the trees and undergrowth.

The woman is very short of breath and when she starts to cough the boy and I look at each other once again. I see the alarm in his eyes now. A crack of distant thunder adds to the intensity of the moment.

"That should do," I say.

We gently put her down on a leaf-littered area between a couple of brush boxes, Bangalows and an ancient beech tree. She coughs some more and now there is a splatter of blood on the edge of her mouth. I am acutely aware that we need to treat this woman right away. I lower my backpack to the ground. The youth is looking into his mother's eyes as if willing her to stay alive. He has not said a word thus far.

"We need to apply pressure and put something around the wound area," I say. He has already taken off his shirt and, despite the heat, has a T-shirt on underneath. I take the portable camping knife out of my pocket, cut the pinstriped shirt into two strips and tear the woman's blouse off her left shoulder. Together we work to wrap the wound tight enough to apply pressure and then carry her the rest of the way – not far to go – to the Meeting Place. Once there, we lay the woman on the ground where months ago I erected a small tarp shelter alongside the quandong tree where the raised platform is. I scramble about and get some antiseptic and pain killers for the woman, as well as water for all of us. I redress the wound with a proper bandage, then go back to get the backpack I slipped out of 10 metres away when it became too heavy. When I return, the woman's breathing is very laboured and she is slipping in and out of consciousness.

"What's your name?" I ask the young man.

He turns his head towards me.

"Fallow," he mouths in a whisper. Or that is what I think he has said.

"Fallow?" I ask.

He nods. Either he is just few on words or he is for the most part unable to speak.

"I'm Sara. This your mother?"

He nods.

The wind is picking up now, branches swaying over our heads. Thunder is creating a distant rolling backdrop. The irony is not lost on me that here I am at last in my catastrophic make-your-own-ending adventure story with every element cranking up the volume as we head towards some sort of climax.

Now what happens? I wonder. I am paralysed for a moment as I look at the man, then his mother and then down the ridge to where more food and supplies wait to be lugged up here. In my confusion, Gale makes an unannounced appearance in my head once again, with the advice that we take care of the woman first, then set her son up to tend to her while I return for the rest of the supplies.

Though not a drop of rain has eventuated, a dust storm is brewing, swirling like a whirling dervish, then punctuated by an unsettling silence between gales. A lone pied butcher bird lands next to the grey tarp on one of the guy ropes and sings a melodious tune that catches the young man's attention as well.

Time stands still.

The cracking of a gum tree branch crashing to the ground nearby puts us in motion again. As if he has read my mind, Fallow sets about securing the tarp and I grab a couple of wool blankets from the metal container. I notice he is very capable not only at throwing rocks but also at tying knots. Together we shift his mother under the tarp, lay her on one blanket and cover her with another. Although it is hot, even here in the shade of the rainforest trees, the woman is shivering, gasping for air, her chest heaving. Her son puts his arms around her as she opens her eyes for a moment and I catch the heart wave that passes between them. It is palpable, I want to drink it in, I want to bathe in it, tender, sweet and knowing. She coughs up some more blood and then, just like that, the life force drains out of her. There is nothing I can do.

I become aware of a buzzing in my ears, my eyesight teeters as I enter that liminal state that occurs when the threshold between life and death has been traversed, a simultaneously palpable and ineffable dimension.

Fallow lays his head in his hands and there is a barely noticeable tremor in his shoulders. I put a hand lightly on his back. I have lost many friends over the years and I was taken from my mother when I was 4 years of age. I haven't seen her since.

"I'll be back," I say when the moment feels right. He looks at me and nods.

I turn back for a moment and see Fallow drop to his knees, his mouth open in anguish, a mournful guttural sound that plunges me into a well of grief I didn't even know existed. Fallow looks at me, or directly into me it feels like, and for a moment I am transported into a hallucination, an altered state of some sort, and I see a young boy, 6 or 7 years of age, with distinctive, straight, long blond hair. He is looking for his mother. Terror. I feel terror now and Fallow sees the shock in my expression when I notice, or maybe I just see it in my mind's eye, that his mouth is barren, he has no tongue. My facial muscles begin to quiver, all senses overwhelmed and I am speechless as I put my left hand to my heart, my eyes locked into his.

I turn to leave once again and I see him shake his head at me but I am listening to my heart racing and I'll be no good to anybody if I don't take a few moments to myself, so I duck my head under some lantana branches and head down the ridge.

# 20    Gale

At night she went to bed hungry, although the peristaltic reaction, that gripping pang in her upper abdomen, had halted after the first few days. She stopped exercising to save her energy, yet she had spent most of the past three days pacing her cell, back and forth. Back and forth. Wracking her brain for a clue as to how to get out of here. On the fourth foodless morning, Gale looked towards the spoon wondering if this metal implement could be of any use. Not that she could dig through concrete. She took the spoon by the water tap to see if it could be used to pry the metal off the wall. The spoon bent. Gale bent over as well in a spasm that twisted through her bowel. Cramped, stuck. Hungry, stumped.

She drifted in and out of hunger and memory lane. She was reliving that time she and Sara had fasted for three days. Lis had, of course, not wanted a bar of it. Gale distinctly remembered her saying, "I love my morning coffee and then a glass of Chablis at night! Why would I want to deprive myself of those pleasures?" That was how it was for Lis. Creature comforts, romantic dreams and going about life without any plans or lofty ideas for the future. Gale was sure Lis had gone along with the Meeting Place merely to hang out with Gale and Sara, and because Lis could envision the creative potential for a real-time dystopian art project. Paradoxically, Lis was passionate about art that captured the preciousness of life in a devastated and threatened landscape, yet she didn't think these things would ever affect her personally. Surely emergency plans were not necessary, not in their lifetimes!

During the floods of 2022, Lis's place had been just high enough to stay safe and sound in the foothills of Lismore Heights. What a great post-flood project she had been able to pull together. Everything was creative fodder, and ultimately Lis thought everything would be fine – the government, technology, business would pull them through these times. In a similar vein, there was no need for a fast or anything that involved deprivation or potential suffering.

Sara and Gale, on the other hand, were keen to detox, to purge the residuals of many a wild party, boozing, eating, sailing through the world in what they had thought in their earlier years was an unbreakable vessel. Their friend Jess from Brisbane had just died of bowel cancer and it swept them into quick action, starting with green smoothies followed by a three-day water-only fast. It had been challenging but the two of them had bantered and whinged their way through the escapade, drawing close together once again. In fact, Gale remembered pulling Sara into her arms and swirling her in a playful jig on their last day, both of them high energy, excited, nearing their goal. They had twirled around Gale's kitchen laughing and giggling, hooting and hollering as they dreamed up what they were going to have for breakfast the next morning.

"Coffee!" Gale called out.

"Toast!" Sara sang.

"Orange juice!"

"Peanut butter, eggs, and strawberries with whip cream!"

Gale had started to lean into Sara's body just a bit more than friends would. She had thought she felt Sara moving closer to her as well.

Gale's mind flitted back and forth. As much as her body had grown sluggish, her mind compensated with delirious activity, running, hiding, escaping from leagues of unknown towering predators. In the wee hours of the morning, she dreamed she was fleeing from faceless men in black uniforms who surrounded her childhood suburban home. Gale crawled through a tunnel, then dropped over a ledge, only to find herself sinking into a dense, confining quicksand-like sludge. Unable to move and gasping for breath, she thrashed about as panic took hold until in the miraculous way of dreams, Gloria, the beagle-labrador cross from her early years, bounced over to her, barking and licking her face, enthusiastically removing dirt from her nostrils and away from her mouth. Her chest heaving, Gale awoke to her cell, to the reality that she was stuck in this concrete box and would die in the next week or two unless food reappeared or she found a way out of this hellhole.

The dream left an imprint on her mind that nudged an old memory to the surface. She must have been three years old. She remembered the sensation that she could not breathe. While the memory was still fuzzy, she sensed that something had been put over her face, a pillow. Yes, in her mind it was her favourite blue checked pillow and suddenly she knew it was her older brother Sam; he was suffocating her. Gale lay on the mattress sweating as she recalled the panic mounting in her body, her small arms thrashing about, as in the dream. She remembered now how Gloey Shmoey, best dog in the world, came to her rescue, barking, licking her face, nudging her with her cold nose, Sam no longer there. Many years later as a young man, Sam took his life and it was Gale who discovered him in his apartment, a needle still hanging from his arm, vomit drooling over blue lips, a chair next to him, with a rope above hanging quietly, unused. His son, Tyler, still an infant, lay in his cot in the room next door.

"Good morning number 87."

"You're still there!"

"How are you feeling today 87?"

"I'm HUNGRY," she yelled. "I need food! What are you doing to us?"

"Thank you. That will be all 87."

Then, as usual, nothing more.

"I need medical attention!" she croaked quietly.

Gale stood in the middle of her cell with both hands thrown up in the air looking towards the speaker as the realisation sunk in that the voice always said the exact same thing. Once a week. Hello 87 and how are you 87 and that will be all. Of course there were more commands in the past, instructions about how the food would be delivered, the announcement of the shower. Yet for weeks now there was nothing new, a mere hello that was probably prerecorded.

She drifted in and out of sleep through the days. She continued to track the passing time with notches on the wall, using dirt from the floor combined with a drop or two of water, as the heavy steel door of the portal kept opening and shutting twice a day. Foodless. She had been in this cell for over two months now. The line between wakefulness and sleep blurred and she dreamed she was tapping through the thick walls with the woman next door. It had become a language, a conversation, like the mysterious coupling of quarks separated across vast distances yet oddly in sync. Immersed in a lucid dream that felt real, Gale noticed a small door, the size of a window under the table between her room and the one next door. She crouched down. Pushed on it. Nothing. She tried again. It wouldn't budge. She noticed a sensor next to the door and held her wrist tech up to it. A small green light blinked and the small door slid open, smoothly tucking itself into the wall out of sight. In the dream, Gale lowered herself onto her belly and began to slither through the small space, arms first. A hand from the other side grabbed her arm and helped her through. For the first time she saw the woman next door clearly, the woman's dark visage twisted awkwardly in grief and ecstasy simultaneously. They fell into each other's arms. They were rolling on the floor, sobbing, nuzzling, murmuring, exclaiming. Hands reached to hands, hips to hips, lips to lips.

"Sara!"

She woke with a start as the imaginary woman next door morphed into the feisty 20-year-old Sara, wearing her favourite red feminist fist T-shirt. Awake now, Gale's body began to heave, wracked with grief and the losses of a lifetime. She wondered where Sara was right now. She could almost sense her out there, somewhere in the bush. Still reeling from the dream, Gale cast an invisible line to Sara, wherever she might be. She wondered if they would ever meet again. Cradling Sara in her mind, Gale's heartbeat eventually slowed as she drifted off to sleep once again. Hold me now, Sara, she whispered to herself as she slipped back into sleep.

Gale woke up to the sound of the portal opening once again, once again an empty tray. She recalled how in her dream the door under the table had opened with her wrist tech and for a moment she wondered if there might be a secret doorway under the table. A quick glance proved her wrong. Snippets from her dream continued to stir the ghosts of her past. She thought back to that time in her twenties when she and Sara had slipped out of Claire's party and ended up kissing each other on the deck. It was passionate, compelling and yet brief, as they had been interrupted by some boisterous friends in search of a smoke. As the joint had made its rounds, Sara disappeared into the party and Gale set off searching from room to room until finally she stumbled across Sara leaving the bathroom with a spunky blond gal – Gale couldn't remember her name although she could certainly remember the sexy miniskirt and black fishnet stockings, boots to kill – the woman and Sara both raucously laughing, arms linked. Gale had reeled backwards, her usually pale cheeks turned to pink as her and Sara's eyes met in a tango. She had wondered if she was too much of a "guy" for Sara, too masculine. Sara was always teasing her about being a boy; maybe they could never be more than friends. Gale had fled the party and within the next few weeks she had met Jeff, solid albeit sedate, with whom she lived for the next ten years until they parted amiably enough five years ago on Gale's thirtieth birthday.

Emmy, with Jeff's red hair and freckled skin but Gale's fit frame, was the gift of their union, hopefully tucked away in Western Australia now.

Today there were no taps back to her from the cell next to hers, no food, no digital voice, no showers, although water still trickled out of the faucet when she pushed the button. She knew she could hasten the dying process if she stopped drinking water. It had been ten foodless days now and Gale was feeling weak and alone.

"Hello, hello! Are you there?" she called out to the woman next door, cautiously at first.

"Anybody there?" she then yelled loudly, and louder yet again.

"Are you there? Heyyyyyy!"

Only silence responded, the concrete walls too thick for her voice to penetrate. Perhaps her tapping friend next door had died. There was not a shred of evidence that the captors were still there. She might be the only one left in the whole building.

She passed the time squeezing puss out of the wound on her wrist. It was something she had done as a child, carefully peeling back a scab when she was alone in her bedroom, overdone in red swirly flowered matching wallpaper, bedspread and blinds. It still made her cringe to this day, the epitome of the feminine box that her mother, father, friends, school, life wanted to enclose her in. Being a girl, and later a woman, had never suited her, she felt a nagging discomfort in the body she was born in. She had always felt more like a boy than a girl, and she would have transitioned away from being identified as a woman long ago had she had the courage to break from family expectations. Instead, she had kept herself hidden. Only Sara knew who she really was. Gale barely even told herself. The role of a woman felt like a corset bound tightly around her soul. She needed to break out of this cell. When she did, she would make major changes in her life. She would start by telling Sara how she really felt about her. She would change her pronoun to 'he' and would start living in her true gender. As a matter of fact, while she still needed to find a way to free herself physically from this cell, she could free her psyche, her soul, her spirit right now. HE could free *his* psyche, *his* soul, *his* spirit right now! Yes, that felt better. Now he could focus on getting out of the cell and finding his friends.

He knew that he was making his wrist worse with the squeezing. Yet the pain was at times a distraction from everything else. The walls. It took him away from the confinement for a moment. The throbbing increased its volume and captivated his attention. A much-needed break from the cell. All his attention focused. Riding waves of pain.

He had self-harmed as an adolescent. That first time, Gale had walked in on Sara, who was cutting crisscross lines on her thigh, a dreamy expression on her face. Gale's initial shock had quickly morphed into curiosity, then something they could try out together, something risky, crossing boundaries, adrenalin.

His thoughts ping-ponged back and forth and he barely moved now to save his energy. He rolled the elastic waistband of his trackies over a couple of times to hold them up. He was getting thin and frail. He would not want to see what he looked like; he had always been meticulously neat and well-tended, yet now his usually short-cropped hazel hair hung twisted and he used his fingers absentmindedly to untangle the brittle knots. He stared at his hands for a moment, the skin dry and cracked, fingers that looked like old, gnarled pointers, blood stains on his right index finger where he had picked at his wrist. Gale walked over to the tap to clean his hands but only a couple drops of water came forth. He pushed the button again. And again. The water no longer flowed. He had to get out of here. Within the next few days.

# 21  Lis

Chloe had vanished. It was one day since Lis's failed mission and the strange encounter with the old woman in the rocking chair. Lis was busy tending to David when she realised that Chloe was nowhere in sight. After a quick look around the house, Lis ran out, her heart fluttering.

Lis turned down Terania Street and spotted Chloe waddling in her drunken way towards the guard station under the overpass. Strangely the guard standing in front of the black vehicle remained unmoving, seemingly paying no attention to the child.

"Chloooooeeeee!" Lis risked calling out softly.

Still the guard did not move, even as Chloe looked momentarily towards Lis and began weaving her way towards a house just to the side. Lis was surprised to see several deer standing casually by the house, grazing on some grasses that did not seem to mind the drought. Lis moved forward, closer to the guard station than she would have dared, and intercepted Chloe at the house, scooping the child up into her arms. She breathed a sigh of relief as she entered the house through the open door, whispering to Chloe that she had scared her half to death, at the same time giving the little girl a good squeeze and a kiss on the head.

Now that she was here, Lis decided to make her way through the house in search of medicines. First to the main bathroom, where there was nothing much that would be of use. She held her breath as she opened the cabinets in the second bathroom, off the master bedroom.

"Got it!" she exclaimed to Chloe.

Doxycycline in one cabinet and amoxicillin in another. She knew David had been treated successfully with amoxicillin another time when he had an ear infection. Lis hurried back to the house, hopeful for the first time in weeks.

# 22 Sara

I empty my backpack of supplies and begin the journey down the ridge to get a load of food and medicines. My heart is racing. I know I probably should stay with the young man but something tells me to leave him to have some solo time with his mother. I can live with this choice. These are unusual times and it is a calamity all around.

I make my way down the ridge to what used to be a gorgeous flowing creek below my place, Leicester Creek, at the headwaters of the Wilsons River, high and fast running during flood season, now only a puddle here and there. I imagine the forest will start to stir as a few raindrops fall but they stop as quickly as they started, unable to do the job. It has been at least three years since we had any good rain, so the forests and the critters who live here have suffered in the extreme. When fires swept the region in 2019, ash fell from the sky as every day the fires swept closer and closer to the southern side of the ranges, threatening everything in their path. My safe place, the rich depths of the lush rainforests, imperilled by Mother Nature herself. With a little help from us humans, of course. Fortunately, these rainforests I am moving through now have enough integrity in them, still resilient enough, after all the punches they have been dealt over the past 100 years, to withstand the flames. That was a terrifying time for all of us and we have always known that it is only a matter of time before the cycle repeats itself. As it is on the verge of doing now. Over time, even these intact forests will lose their capacity to withstand such huge weather changes. I am surprised that I have not woken to smoky skies over these past months, until today, when even as a lone raindrop falls on my nose I can also smell the all-too-familiar biting scent of smoke.

I arrive at the dusty basin and pause for a moment to sit on a large smooth rock that I know well, where I tune into the presence of Creek Aunty, a larger-than-life Aboriginal woman, an energy I have met in the past, always there for me when I am in trouble. She holds me in her arms as a few more drops roll down my cheeks, enticing me to lick my lips, then tilt my head back anticipating sweet beads of precious water dripping directly into my mouth. For a moment I am lost in sensation, a misty shower comes through and that distinct moist earthy smell in the air is powerful. Petrichor. Delicious. Like my first acid trip, I inhale deeply, eyes half closed, transported for just one moment, a tiny speck on a pulsing planet that is speeding through space in our corner of a spiral galaxy.

With the speed of light, I am snapped back into the present by a low gravelly voice.

"There she is Jim," a man rasps.

I turn towards the voice. It is the man I saw down at Paul's place, thin and wiry, slightly bent over, rifle pointed directly at my chest.

"Well, well, well. Who do we have here?" the other man growls at me with a twisted tone that sends chills up my spine. I startle, jump, as I feel the nose of his rifle jabbing at my lower back.

"Don't move or I'll blow your fucking guts out," he snarls as the weapon drops lower and pushes pointedly against my buttocks.

I freeze. My body is so tense now that it is almost unbearable. My head starts to cloud, I fear I am going to pass out. I hold still as instructed and stifle the cry that wants to come out. For a moment I am back in my repeating perpetrator dream. The realisation snaps my mind into a crisp awareness; Ninja-Sa has been training for this moment for the last few decades. I silently repeat Ninja-Sa! in my mind and with this declaration I carefully shift my body to a taut and alert position as I quickly assess the situation. One man with a gun behind me, one in front. Nowhere to escape to. I fend off the habitual sink into despair and instruct myself to look for the opportunity, further up the track perhaps, where I know the hidden wallaby tracks that wind through the leggy lantana that still survives in large patches. I need to be patient like a hunter, not that I know much about that, but I do know about being around wild creatures and these men have a savageness that I wouldn't want to mess with. All this flashes through my mind as the man behind me tells me to slowly turn around.

"And no funny business!" he barks.

# 23   Gale

There was no water to wash his hands or face with these past two days. The cell was hot as a dry sauna, every inch coated by a nose-wrinkling stench that ballooned from the drop toilet. Gale breathed through pursed lips as much as possible. He was dying of hunger and an infection in his arm that sent waves of edgy sensation coursing through his body.

In desperation, Gale peered down the toilet while he held his breath. Although he weighed less than 50 kilos now, reduced to the size he was as a thirteen -year-old, Gale didn't think his hips and shoulders would fit down the metal pipe. He gagged at the thought of the slurry of shit and piss that would await below in absolute darkness where rodents bathed in luxury. Gale dry heaved and clenched his fists. The ultimate test of claustrophobia. He was relieved that this was not a feasible escape route.

Twice a day, the portal continued to open and shut, open and shut, it was the only thing that marked the days. No more voice and the ceiling light no longer glowed. Gale sat in the dark by the opening of the portal, sweating and dazed. He waited for hours for the small metal door to slide open so he could have a careful look. Even if he could jam the door on his side to stop it from closing, he was doubtful he could squeeze through the shelf area and out the other side. He put his hands into the portal to fully check it out and found it was only as wide as the cafeteria tray and half as high again in height. If he could hold both sides open, he could try to get an arm or a leg to the other side but he didn't think he had the flexibility to contort his body to squeeze through in some masterful feat of yoga. After checking it out again at the afternoon mealtime, a plan hatched. The food portal was just to the left of the door to the cell. If he could reach his left arm through the opening to the other side, he might be able to reach up and scan his wrist-tech over the sensor used to get back into the cell like he did after the exercise regimes. He could use his tray to jam his side of the sliding door open.

He didn't know if the metal screen on the other side would slide up if he had his side jammed. There was only one way to find out. For the first time in weeks, he felt a glimmer of hope that wrapped itself around the twisting hunger in his belly as he tried to get some sleep. He awoke early, alert, restless, mouth parched, and by repeatedly pushing the button he managed to squeeze a couple drops of water out of the faucet. The heat in the room did its work on his body, moving sweat down his armpits and his chest. Gale used fingers and tongue to lap up what he could, sucking any moisture he could find.

After what seemed like a lifetime, the portal finally slid open on his side and Gale positioned the tray sideways to hold the gap ajar. The faint smell of smoke met his nostrils as he manoeuvred his arm onto the shelf. The portal was at waist height and he would have to lean into it if his plan was to work so he rolled up his mattress and placed it beneath his knees to give him the leverage he needed. At most he would be able to squeeze his arm through and possibly part of his head. He would not be able to worm his whole body through to the other side, yet he was hopeful he could thread his arm and twist it up to where his wrist would meet the scanner. It was a long 15 minutes waiting for the back to lift. A slight whirr. Gale held his breath. Worried the back would not slide open if the front were still open. He pushed the thought away. He was in the familiar territory of logic and a calmness descended like when he was immersed in the thick of a complicated flowchart. Some creative thinking might be needed, although there did not appear to be many options. The back panel began to lift and Gale squeezed his arm through, his head laying on its side where the tray usually sat. He could just manage to move his hand and wrist through to the other side. His heart sank. his hand could not reach far enough and the back panel was closing on him. He had nothing more to hold it open so he placed the tray back on the shelf and withdrew. The smell of smoke wafted forebodingly into his cell, bringing haunting memories of the 2019 bushfires.

Gale knew what he had to do. It was his only chance and it needed to happen quickly as he was not only hungry and battling infection but also dying of thirst, his lips cracked in lines, his mouth and eyes parched. He had only urinated twice that day, a strong-smelling liquid that he had directed into his cup. He wasn't sure whether drinking your own urine would help or not. Hadn't he heard of someone in China surviving in a mine shaft by drinking his own pee? He knew it would also contain the waste products being flushed from his system. In any case, he had given it a go that morning but barely managed to drink a mouthful of the liquid, the pungent smell of ammonia accosting him like week-old cat litter.

Gale had an idea but it would take some precision and steadiness. He braced himself as he realised he would need to dig the wrist-tech chip out of his festering wound. The plan was to hold the small chip between his fingers and then he would be able to reach up that much higher to where the sensor was located. Hopefully. He knew exactly where the chip was located; he had felt around for it many times as he pushed down on the small circle of a wound. He would need to excavate through the yellowish pus that he had been squeezing daily in hopes of keeping the infection at bay but more so for lack of anything better to do while time had slowed to an endless desert. Gale's fingernails had grown long over the past couple of months. He glanced up at his notches. Over nine weeks he had been here now. He took to the task in a delirium through the night, gnawing at his thumb, index and middle fingernails with the desperation of a rodent chewing its way out of a trap. He shaped and sharpened his keratin tools until he was ready to begin the operation, poking at his skin, prying the wound open. In the end, he used his teeth as well, biting, and picking, working away at gaining access.

When the wound was gaping, he used the metal spoon to push down in an attempt to dislodge the chip. The room began to spin around him and he steeled himself, He detested the sensation of blood draining out of his head, as if the lights were being extinguished in his brain. It would not be the first time. He had passed out many times as a younger person, seeing his brother come home with blood pouring out of his left eye and cheek after he got into a fight at school. Knees buckled, Gale had hidden inside the closet until his mother whisked Sam off to hospital. And then that time Gale and his family were in a massive pile-up on the freeway. As a parent he had been forced to get over his queasiness around blood. Emmy coming home, her mangled fingers dangling from a few threads of tendons and ligaments. A nasty accident with the paper guillotine. Gale pushed the images out of his head. Not helpful.

He steadied himself and pried the wound open once more and could see the microchip now. Known as a mote in IT land, there would be no battery, no power required, and a unique identifier. Usually they were no bigger than a grain of rice but this mote might be somewhat bigger since it had an additional feature, the ability to paralyse the nervous system. He had no idea how it did so, something that was no doubt developed for military use. He used the edge of the table to hold the wound apart and gave the spoon a good push to pry the mote out. Sharp nerve pain tore up his arm, nausea overwhelmed his senses.

Gale came to, lying face down on the concrete floor amidst a small amount of spew and a bump he could feel on his head. He squinted at the wound and could see the gold-coloured chip had been dislodged, emerging like the head of a newborn. Once again, he held the wound open with the edge of the table and using his hand and mouth, teeth and tongue, Gale succeeded in extracting the chip, the size of a small navy bean. He closed his eyes, his back against the wall, exhausted, sweating and feverish.

Gale dozed off and on. Delirious and yet alert to the sound of the portal opening. He needed to be ready when it opened again. He carefully held the chip in his right hand resting on his lap. While the rest of him slept, his ears continued to listen for the tones that habitually sounded before each meal, even after there was no longer any food. He worried he would not be awake and continued to wrench himself out of the depths of exhaustion, readying the chip between his fingers, picturing himself reaching up to the sensor located up the wall.

When the tone finally announced the opening of the portal, Gale was ready. He quickly pushed the tray into place to hold the front open and waited fifteen minutes until the back opened as well, when usually the tray would be picked up. Once again, the acrid smell of smoke infiltrated the cell. Gale shoved his arm through the opening and pushed his head in alongside his shoulder. He reached up and waved the chip around. It began to slip out of his fingers and panic propelled him back out of the manoeuvre into the cell. This was his last chance and he could not afford to drop the mote. He searched around for an idea to keep it glued to his fingers. He could undo the threads on his trackies and wind it around his middle finger for maximum length. Too hard. He would give this one more go. He needed to stay steady despite the shakiness in his body. Gale held the chip between thumb and index finger and once again thrust himself through the opening. This time he carefully pictured where the sensor was located and pried and pushed his way around in the small opening until he could feel the ID scanner along the adjacent wall with his middle finger. His shoulder was jammed tightly in the gap and he held his breath as if to make himself smaller. Gale carefully waved his fingers with chip held tightly in front of the sensor. Perhaps it was no longer operational, he wondered.

Nothing occurred for a moment. Then door 87 swung open. Gale slumped to the floor and crawled towards the opening. The heat and smell of smoke greeted him like an old friend.

# 24   Sara

With one foul-smelling scrawny man a couple of metres in front and the other breathing down my back, we make our way up the track towards my place. Down here there are still some trees and shade and the track is overgrown with farmers' friend, scotch thistle, dwarf amaranth, billygoat weed and the like. I am thinking ahead to one of the side tracks I carved out of a hefty lantana patch with my machete just a few weeks ago. I wonder if I were to quickly dive down that trail if I might be able to escape these rough hounds or be shot in the back and left to die like roadkill.

"Keep going bitch," the man behind me growls and pokes me with his rifle in the small of my back. I wince and feel my stomach contract, giving rise to my old friends, Doubt and Despair. I won't be able to escape these men. I will be abused and imprisoned. There is no way I can find safety. Catastrophic thinking swamps my mind in a quagmire of confusion that sends me back into childhood trauma once again. I take a breath into my diaphragm and work at making myself clear and focused. I pick up my pace to keep in time with the man who is leading the way. I tell myself to wait for the right moment to present itself. Don't panic, I think, as a few scant drops of rain alight on my cheeks and nose. I use my tongue to taste the sky's offering and it soothes me in a visceral way.

We are nearing the hidden side track that could be my escape route. I know it is high risk but I am starting to panic at the thought of these men taking me home with them. I am thinking I would rather die than find myself in that position ever again. Just as we round the corner where I have cleared beyond the lantana, I count down in my head – three, two, one – then throw myself through the lantana to the track beyond.

"Not so fast!" the man trailing behind me yells out and I feel the whack of his rifle against my calf as his knobby hand grabs my boot. Both men are now pulling me back, dragging me face downwards, lantana scratching my cheeks and eyes. They are shouting with rage as they turn me over onto my back, and one of them pins me down by the arms, the other by the feet. I can feel myself losing touch with my body, I am about to lose consciousness. My worst nightmare. About to happen here, only this time to my adult body. I cannot bear it. I fade away.

I am fading, falling from consciousness. Shots ring out as I come to, a blur of voices, panic and then pain in my leg. I hear one of them swear, then his arms, shoulders, chest and head fall heavily on top of my neck and face. I fear I am going to suffocate and I scramble out from under him. I hear the man who is still standing shouting out to someone.

"What the fuck! Where did you come from?"

I lift my head slightly just as a rock the size of a golf ball hits the man dead centre between the eyes, a resounding bullseye. He crumples to the ground like a cartoon character, a moaning heap of diminishing expletives. I lift my gaze and see Fallow standing tall and erect on the track, unharmed, approaching me now after he grabs the unconscious man's rifle.

"But how did you do that?" I wonder aloud as relief floods through my every cell. I start to cry but then I am laughing uncontrollably, hysterical, as I lie on the track, hands to the ground, my nails digging into the dirt, holding on for dear life. Shortly, I get a grip on myself, take a deep breath.

"Thank you Fallow," I murmur, my mouth unable to form further words as I am stunned at this young person who has miraculously saved me. Fallow is hovering over me now where I lie on the ground and together we have a look at my shin. The skin is broken and it is swollen red and looking angry but this I can tolerate as a trade-off for the violence that was about to happen to me. I reassemble my limbs and body into a standing position and my eyes move to Fallow's arm where a stream of blood is now coursing down his arm.

"You're hurt!" I exclaim. He lifts the arm of his T-shirt and it turns out a bullet has grazed him but nothing that my first aid kit can't fix up. We stand side by side, Fallow and I. He is looking one way down the track towards the bush while I look up the other to where I have more food supplies hidden and even further along to where my shack is. The man who was on top of me appears to be dead, the other one begins to groan and flail his arms. Fallow and I look at each other.

"What should we do?" I whisper.

I am tempted to put this man down as you would an injured animal, put him out of his misery, ours as well. Our safety. While I am thinking these thoughts, Fallow kneels by the man's side and takes some rope out of his small knapsack. He expertly ties the man's arms behind his back. Fallow moves swiftly and competently and, as I look at him now,

I realise I might have still underestimated his age. He now looks to be in his early to mid-twenties, a young man who evidently has quite a few skills up his sleeve.

"My place is just up the track, a bit further," I say as he urges the man up onto his feet. The man is still dazed and moving slowly but I am worried he could turn on us at any moment. I grab the dead man's rifle from the ground and switch roles. Now it is me who is armed and walking behind the prisoner, this person who just moments ago wanted to rape and humiliate me. I feel my eyes burning with rage for a moment, my finger twitching on the trigger. Fallow turns his head back to look at me at just that moment and gently shakes his head.

"Let's get him to my place and then we can go back up the range to lay your mother to rest," I suggest.

Fallow nods his agreement. I see the pain in his eyes at the mention of his mother.

"Not a word out of you," I say to the man under my breath. "Walk, don't talk."

The man complies. I imagine he is concussed and his forehead would be screaming with pain judging from the bump that is loudly protruding now.

We walk up the track just past where I hid all the supplies yesterday. Was it just yesterday? Fallow and I stop in our tracks as we hear voices coming from up above at the property. Maybe it could be Gale or Pot or someone from the community.

"You stay here, with him," I say to Fallow and nod towards the injured man whose eyes stare at the ground, dazed. "I'll go have a look."

Fallow shakes his head in disagreement.

"You want to come with me?" I ask, puzzled.

"No," he mouths, "not safe." He shakes his head and his eyes move in an arc towards the land atop. He puts his hand on my arm lightly and I realise he has a gift of some sort, an intuition, a knowing. He did find me even though I left him up in the bush with his mother. He seems to know where danger lurks. Inside of me Ninja-Sa gives a little chuckle for a moment, a fellow superhero amid the Armageddon.

"Not safe then up ahead, eh?" I say and he nods. I suggest that we leave the man with his arms tied and send him on his way towards the property while we keep the rifle trained on his back.

"No turning around, not a peep out of you," I snarl at him and we send him off.

After he disappears over the hilltop, Fallow and I turn around and head back to the supply station, where we load up both our packs and head towards the Meeting Place once again to tend to his mother's body and put it in the ground. Out of nowhere, Boots appears and rubs against my sore shin, purring. She has become much friendlier these past weeks as I have become quite the provider of food and shelter.

As we head back up the ridge, the drops of rain stop and are just as easily forgotten. The land quickly resumes the familiar flavour of hardened dryness. I gaze up at the sky and it foretells no further offerings. Drought is stubborn and relentless; once it gets a foothold, it is loath to give it up. I am lifted out of my musings by the dreaded smell of smoke. I glance up to the eastern ridge across the valley on the other side of the road by our farm and I see the hazy skies in the distance. If the fire descends the ridge it will need to be stopped at the dirt road before it jumps over onto our land. Or what has been our land for a short while, Bundjalung Country forever. I wonder if whoever is on the land now will know how to fight the fire up by the road.

I consider the risks of returning to the property. We could join forces, be allies in firefighting. Mutual interests and all. Historically everybody comes together around bushfires and other disasters, other than the government. If a fire were to jump the road, the properties would be demolished and whoever is there would probably head down to the creek and into the bush, seeing as the guards are at the end of our road. These intruders might know a way out. They must have come in somehow past the guard stations but otherwise they might look to the ranges as a good option, the rainforests that are still intact and stretch for hundreds of kilometres to the north. I don't want to be up there with everybody surging through in a panic. Which all goes to say that I'd better head back down in the next couple of days and see about making contact.

It has already been a long day when we begin taking turns with the shovel to dig a hole where we will lay Fallow's mother to rest. The ground is hard and unrelenting in its resistance. Now and then we look at each other across the silence. I can see the raw heartbreak in Fallow's oceanic eyes and I am sure he can see fear percolating in mine as I think about whoever has taken over our land. The smell of smoke takes up residence in our nostrils and on our clothing, adding an eerie blanket over the rainforest. While floods and rainstorms made for difficult times a few years back, bushfires bring abject terror. Especially for those like me who have always seen the forest as a refuge, a safe place to retreat. Even as a young girl I found safety in the little patch of trees I could locate while I was shuffled from one home to another, relatives at first, foster care later. If there was only one tree, I would climb up and mingle with the large branches that soothed me knowingly, the sap murmuring to my veins, relaxing every cell in my body. I head up to sit on the platform now as I am clearly in need of just that. Fallow sits under the brushbox next to his mother's grave. Eventually he joins me. A lone pigeon is wom-pooing in the distance. It is a familiar melody that I can sink into. We sit. And sit some more. The rattle and buzz of the cicadas form a deafening and electrifying backdrop.

I descend from the tree to open a can of baked beans to heat up and cook some white rice on the camp stove I have set up. We eat at dusk, our appetites beleaguered by the heaviness of the hot dry air. I am slightly calmed to see Boots casually slink into the camp, where she nonchalantly enjoys the bounty. After the meal, Fallow and I lie at opposite sides of the platform, a mozzie net over us. My mind is once again a whirling tornado. Fire is much too close for comfort. After all our preparations, all my many visits to this place over the years, I reluctantly admit that what was the ultimate

Meeting Place is no longer the place of choice. We always knew we needed a multiplicity of options, several land options and ideally a motorhome ready for a quick getaway. Still, it is difficult for me to face the fact that it is probably best if we head to town. At least we might find Gale and Lis there. The cynic in me says that is highly unlikely and I don't even let myself think about Pot just now. I bemoan the fact that we never put in place a UHF handheld radio system to communicate with each other when all other comms went down. I am thinking we should go to Gale's place nearer the coast; yes, that would be the best option for now. Images of the ocean soothe my mind, my eyelids become heavy.

"I'm thinking of the ocean," I whisper to Fallow. "The waves, the salt water, the open expanse," I murmur. Eventually we fall into a slumber, both of us completely exhausted.

# Part 6 Round-up Week 10

## August 2028

# 25 Gale

Shocked. Gale stood still as stone until the click click of the door ceased to reverberate. For a moment he hesitated, unsure whether he would get zapped if he attempted to cross the threshold. With the chip no longer implanted he reassured himself that this was no longer possible. The only sound he could hear was the thump of his heartbeat. Stealthily he put one step in front of the other as he edged towards the door.

"Can I go through?" he beseeched the ceiling.

When there was no response, he put one finger through the doorway, testing the waters as if it were an electric fence. Take it easy. Don't run. There may be a guard waiting just outside. He coached himself despite the panic that careened wildly through his cellular body.

Three small tentative steps and he was standing by the doorway. Gale cast his gaze beyond as he leaned over to look from side to side. He couldn't see anybody. He moved his left hand towards the threshold, poked his index finger first, then his whole hand and arm, through the doorway. Still no signs of life. He lifted his left leg gingerly, waved it through the doorway and carefully lowered his foot to the concrete floor, like someone walking tentatively through a long-abandoned minefield. When there was no reaction, Gale inhaled deeply and just like that he walked out into the corridor where hands on hips he surveyed the scene. Absolute stillness. In the corner he saw one of the guards, slumped, immobile in the corner.

"Hello?" he croaked.

The guard made no movement. He could see that it was inoperative, lying at an odd angle, no apparent life in its eyes. Gale moved next door to number 88 and tried to open the door with the microchip still gripped tightly between his thumb and index finger but the door did not budge and there was no response when he called out. He strode over to the exit sign where the stairs were located and this door too would not open. Without hesitation Gale walked towards the guard. He had always been fascinated by all things technical.

"Sorry," he said as he propped the guard up against the wall and removed the well-ironed button-down khaki shirt from one side of its body. When the arm to the shoulder was revealed, he had no time to marvel at the human likeness of the flesh. A careful look at the arm where it met the shoulder and he found what he was looking for. A small silver bead protruded from a hole at the top of the tricep, where there was a thin seam between the arm and the shoulder. Gale pushed the bead in, twisted the arm until it released itself from the rest of the body and then swiftly detached the different coloured wires that still held it in place. He was assuming the chip was in the wrist, implanted in the same way everyone else's was. The guards had been factory manufactured and could be dismantled for repairs as easily as they had been put together.

Gale carried the arm over to the exit and held the wrist up to the sensor. The door released and he was free to go. As he looked up the stairs, stars floated briefly in front of his eyes and he lowered his head below his knees to fend off another fainting spell. After his head cleared, Gale headed down the eight flights, staying in the stairwell. He was weak and parched, overheated, and the smell of smoke was strong.

When he arrived at the ground floor, he exited into the waiting room where he and the others had arrived that first day. Gale reeled with dizziness that sent a shudder spasming through his bowels. He needed to locate food and water. He looked around and to his right he saw the hallway that led to the medical room he had been taken to. To his left was a second hallway with three unopened doors. He used the robot arm to open the first. It clicked open like the others and he put his hand on the round metal doorknob, paused for a moment and then turned it clockwise. Gale leapt back with a yelp. There was movement in the room. He fought the urge to slam the door and stood stock still. No sign of anything.

"Hello?" he called out tentatively. "Anybody there?"

Gale's eyes crept cautiously around the doorway. In just moments, his pupils adjusted to the dimness and revealed his own image reflected in a wall-to-wall mirror that lined the back of the room. He stared aghast at his mid-length dishevelled hair and the protruding cheek bones that etched hollows of strain on his face. He barely recognised himself. He entered the room and looked towards the metal shelves that lined the walls. They were filled with clothing, everything he was familiar with: track pants, T-shirts, hoodies, socks, sneakers. The rest of the room was filled with a few card tables and foldable chairs like the ones in the waiting room. Nothing else as far as he could see. No people, no food.

Gale walked back outside into the hall and proceeded to the next door to the left. He opened the door and his body again shot backwards as a putrid odour assailed his senses, the omnipresent smoky smell giving way to that of death and decay. Gale's nose and cheeks squished together as he looked into the room and allowed his eyes to adjust once more. He could just make out a series of chunky ankle straps bolted to the floor and there in the corner he could see the body of what appeared to have been a young woman with ankle bolted, curled up in a foetal position. The woman wore the same clothing as Gale but her head was shaved of hair. The foul odour propelled Gale backwards and he pulled the door quickly shut, retreating to the hallway.

Gale's heart was racing as he proceeded to the third room. He thought for a moment of Sara, who had dragged him along to a cult place in Bali one year for a "Shake-It-Off" retreat that involved tobacco-smoking rituals interspersed with snacking on psychedelic mushrooms. Sara would probably suggest he do that shaking thing now but there was no time and no tobacco anywhere in sight, let alone food or water. Gale let his breath release in a whoosh and for a few seconds allowed the tremors to pass through his body. He pictured Sara bopping like a drugged-up teenager at a rock concert.

He cautiously opened the last door. His jaw dropped and he swiftly entered the room. He had hit the jackpot. Shelves from floor to ceiling were loaded with tin cans sporting colourful labels touting "Synth Meat", along with trays, bowls and mugs, and a makeshift kitchen cooktop and pot. His eyes beelined to the 15-litre water cooler bottle that sat casually in the corner and boxes upon boxes of half-litre bottles of water. Gale grabbed a cup and guzzled 3 cups of the liquid, warm in the heat of the room. To Gale it was water he would remember for the rest of his life. He did not notice the tears streaming down his cheeks as he snatched one of the cans and pried it open by its ring-pull top. Then grasping a spoon from a plastic box, he scooped up the contents and gulped down several spoonfuls before willing himself to slow down as he began to choke on the gluggy substance. His stomach had shrunk to the size of a pea and he was quickly satiated.

Gale headed back to the waiting room and towards the exit that led back outside to where they had been dropped off that day many months ago. He clicked open the door with the guard arm, stepped onto the concrete pad where they had been corralled when they first arrived. He stood still, dazzled to be outside once again. Ash floated down onto his head and the smell of smoke was strong, denser than any he had experienced in past bushfire seasons.

He glanced around at the familiar mesh that wrapped itself around the fence, then took a step towards the final gate to freedom when the taps from the cell next door rapped in his mind. He knew he needed to head back inside and see if Number 88 and the other women in the building could be rescued. Yet he hesitated at the threshold. Sweat streamed down his cheeks as his stomach twisted in knots with the food he had shovelled in. The dryness of the outside air against his already chapped lips made him squint his eyes and take in the hazy sky above. Now that he had the guard arm, he knew he could open the other doors in the building. Gale turned and headed back into the building.

After taking a hoodie from the clothing room, Gale headed into the kitchen area where he grabbed a couple of cans of food and bottles of water and put them into the hoodie for easy carrying, then slowly ascended to the top floor, the tenth, stopping now and then to wait for his head to clear of the dizziness that overwhelmed him. Every door on the floor opened easily and to his surprise each room was empty of inhabitants. The same on the ninth floor. Gale was anxious to return to his floor to open door 88, where the only person he had communicated with over the past months in prison might still be alive, although it had been a week since any taps had been returned from next door.

Aside from Gale's door, all the others on the eighth floor were shut. Gale opened the doors one by one and found that they too were empty. With heaviness in his heart, he held the guard arm up to number 88, heard the familiar click, then twisted and pulled the door open. He gasped. Standing there looking straight at him and equally startled stood a woman with clothing hanging off her hungry body and long wavy hair tumbling down over her hunched shoulders. This woman was younger than Gale, mid-20s probably. Her deep brown eyes met Gale's grey ones. Both screamed but Gale only heard his own voice. No sound came out of the woman's wide-open mouth.

The woman raced past Gale into the hallway weaving erratically, first this way and then the other. Gale spun around.

"It's okay, it's okay," he called out, his voice scratchy. "There's nobody else here."

The woman turned and faced Gale, who took one of the cans of food, opened it and placed it and a spoon on the floor in front of the woman, a bottle of water next to it. Gale then moved back towards the corner of the hallway where the armless guard still sat slumped against the wall, giving the tapper woman plenty of space. The woman lunged towards the bottle and downed the water in several gulps. She then dug down with her fingers into the canned food.

In her haste, she sliced her hand on the edge of the can without appearing to notice. Fully absorbed in eating, she paid no attention to Gale whatsoever. He had fleetingly imagined the two of them might find themselves talking rapidly and planning next steps but he could see now that this was not about to happen. Gale approached the woman where she knelt on the hard floor with one hand steadily making its way to the bottom of the can. He was cautious as the woman exuded untethered wildness, moving her body in erratic ways.

"I'm Gale."

The woman dropped the can to the floor and glanced sideways at Gale, her features distorted in anguish. She went limp and sat in a lumpy heap on the floor.

"Let's get some water downstairs and clean up that cut on your hand, then find a way out of here."

The throbbing from Gale's arm reminded him that he too needed a clean-up. Hopefully there would be a supply cabinet in the medical room to help with the infection.

"Let's get your shoes on first," Gale said but the woman did not seem to hear and sat unblinking.

Gale murmured soothingly as he approached the woman and guided her to her feet by the elbow. As he began to lead her towards her cell to get her shoes, the woman pulled away, a look of horror contorting her face as it dawned on her that they were headed back into her cell. She ran towards the stairwell, the exit door still slightly ajar from when Gale had come through. Gale went into the woman's cell, grabbed the shoes and then went back into the hallway and followed her down the stairs.

"Hey wait!" Gale called out.

# 26  Lis

Days had passed, or was it weeks, Lis couldn't be certain. By some miracle the antibiotics had done the job and David was finally on the mend and moving about the house, playing with Chloe once again, albeit with a languid lethargy. Lis was rolling words around on her tongue like "languid", "lethargic", "listless". She too felt lacklustre, the dense heat and cloaking smell of smoke making it difficult to muster much energy for the day.

She could smell the rotten-egg odour emanating from the almost empty gas bottle. They were running out of drinking water, they had used their last sheet of toilet paper and the pantry was almost bare except for a sack of rice and some canned beans and tomatoes that remained. They could raid other houses; however, she dreaded moving about in the streets for fear of the guards or other marauders. She knew they needed to get a move on things but felt uncertain about whether to head out to Sara's or make their way back to her house and then maybe to Gale's. Yesterday she could see smoke to the north and to the west.

As was her habit, before breakfast Lis slipped out to see if all was as usual. Wags came along, as was his habit, to merrily sniff his way through the bush and guide Lis from one yard to the next but this morning he broke into a trot as they left the house, beelining straight for the intersection where the guard station was set up. Lis ducked behind a scraggly hedge along the side of the paved road. She had grown very attached to this gentle bundle of joy, as had Chloe and David. Wags was barking excitedly now. She thought she heard peals of laughter punctuated by a hacking cough, then loud bantering and shouts. Wags came bounding back doing his special happy dance, very pleased with his discovery. She could hear teases and taunts; it sounded like fun and games over there. She took a deep breath and widened her eyes. Perhaps she had floated off into a daydream, a bit of wishful thinking.

"Rooff Rooff!" Wags barked at her, bringing her back to attention. He moved towards the guard station and then looked back at her, coaxing her to join him. Lis followed tentatively.

"What!?" She exclaimed aloud at the sight of people. Other than the bizarre encounter with the woman sitting outside in the rocking chair, she had not interacted with anyone other than David and Chloe for quite some time. Lis moved slowly towards the intersection and stopped some metres away.

"Woop woop, yo man, look at these moves bro!" A young dark-skinned man appeared to be dancing with one of the uniformed guards in his arms.

"Let's give him a bit of a bash up, see if he likes that," the other lad roused. He was a wiry fair-skinned fella with a baseball cap, who Lissy recognised as the one she had almost bowled over the day she had fled the supermarket. Same sneakers and blue jeans with holes in the knees barely held up below his hips where boxers revealed themselves.

Lis moved forward now as the first youth took the guard and laid him over his knee as if to wallop him old-fashioned style.

"Use his taser," the baseball cap called out just as they took note of Lissy's arrival.

"Hey," they both muttered, casual, as if this were an everyday encounter at an everyday event.

"Hi," Lis said. "The guard's not a real person?" Shocked.

"Naah!" exclaimed the dark-haired, good-looking youth with a faint pencil-thin moustache. He took the arms and bent them backwards to demonstrate, then took the head and began to twist at it as if it were a bottle cap.

"What are you two doing?"

"Nuttin," replied the baseball cap.

"Any sign of other people?"

"Not really. We spotted you a couple days ago over in the house at the corner. Saw your boy slipping across the street."

"David?"

"Guess."

"Where are your families?"

They shrugged. But she knew the answer. Gone with the rest of them.

"You haven't seen my daughter? Sal?"

Shook their heads.

"Just that old guy down by the bridge."

"And a few others around town this morning on our way here."

"Yeh, true."

"Got any tobacco, sis?" The baseball cap youth lit up a rollie, his words coming out in staccato as he exhaled.

"What? No! Don't you want to find your families? You're just wandering around having fun?"

The two young men looked down at the ground.

"Hey Chazz, let's go find a feed at Eli's mum's place. Her pantry was always loaded."

"Yeh, good idea."

And with a barely perceptible nod to Lis, their long legs sauntered off, leaving the guard lying in an unnatural position, head turned backwards, one arm twisted sideways. One of the lads returned and quickly grabbed the helmet and jacket. The other already had the taser.

Wags lay casually on the ground, nose between his legs, heavily engrossed in some routine grooming.

Lis pondered the simplicity of the boys' lives as well as the retriever's. They seemed to not have a worry in the world, except where to score their next smoke or, in Wags' case, his next meal. Lis took a closer look around her now. There was only one vehicle, a boxy black truck, a metal foldable chair and the remains of the guard, apparently a mere robot. Lis remembered seeing a current affairs show sometime last year about the robo-guards, how they were policing the prison systems now as well as the quarantine facilities and off-shore refugee camps and were being trialled in city neighbourhoods where violence was on the rise.

Lis wondered what had caused the robot to shut down after all this time. Maybe too little solar power because of the smoke or maybe it had been remotely shut down. Some kind of control headquarters in Sydney perhaps? Lis's mind was sliding in all directions like a car skidding through a mud patch. Her eyes lifted towards the centre of town where she could see smoke billowing there as well as to the north and to the west. They had better get a move on. Maybe with no robo-guards left, Sal had been able to return home and now that the guards were no longer operable, perhaps she and her family could head in whatever direction they liked.

# 27 Sara

At dawn, above the cacophony of the cicadas, I hear the howling of wild dogs in the distance. Just last year, several people were attacked up here in the Border Ranges when they were out on solo expeditions and I am wary of a hungry pack. I slip down from the platform and take a short jaunt up to the ridge road where I know there is a gap nearby that will give me a clear view down to our property below. As I head up the last few metres, I am breathing heavily thanks to the extra weight I am carrying from days of peanut butter, popcorn and endless variations of pasta. Ironic to be in the apocalypse looking like an overweight consumer, the epitome of all that has gone wrong in this century.

Peering through the gap in the brushbox stand, I can see streaks of movement below. Where did all these people come from, I wonder. They are running around in the paddocks, driving about in old utes and trying to put out the fire that is burning on the ridge just across the road. I've been told that earlier on Bundjalung people would have performed slow cold burns routinely, this being a walking path that moved across country, from Tweed Heads down south to Grafton. Now it looks like a fast hot burn is racing through where the trees and shrubs have all dropped their withered, desiccated leaves to the hardened ground no longer covered by grasses. Like a fuse dipped in diesel ripping across the land. Soon the people down below will be looking to escape and will head up this way or at least down to the creek to avoid the guard station down the end of the road. From my vantage point I am shocked to see the property next door to ours is in flames. My eyes widen with horror but there is no time for tears. The past ten years of my life will soon go up in smoke. It is time to move and I head back down to the Meeting Place.

"We need to go," I tell Fallow, who I notice is already gathering supplies, the men's rifles included, and putting them in his backpack.

I cannot find Boots, although I call for her. Strangely it is this feral creature that at this moment I feel sad about leaving. We also abandon Fallow's mother's burial site as we head down the road and out of the park. I tense in anticipation of a guard post when we get down onto the paved roads below but Fallow seems nonplussed, relaxed even, as he saunters along with his hands in his pockets, his shoulders slightly slouched.

"Move with the land[1]." For a moment I think Fallow has spoken but then I realise this voice sits upright in my mind as we set course to retreat from the forests, the fires and the violence. Something stirs within me as if a reassuring hand has been extended towards me and cuts through my panic. I can almost hear Gale laughing at me at the same time.

"Sara, only you would be having a spiritual epiphany just as you are fleeing your home in terror!"

---

[1] "Move with the land. Maintain diverse languages, cultures and systems that reflect the ecosystems of the shifting landscapes you inhabit over time." —T. Yunkaporta, *Sand Talk: How Indigenous Thinking Can Save the World,* 2019

I smile and look at Fallow, who must see the glint in my eyes. I imagine he has heard the voice too but the moment interrupted as a couple of small planes roar by overhead. My heartbeat quickens as I know only the authorities have aircraft or fuel at this point, aside from a few canisters here and there like we stored down below on the community. The skies have been empty these past months and these carriers are likely not flying over to help put out the bushfires. I can't see their markings and I realise I have left my glasses behind at the Meeting Place and now it is too late to retrieve them. I can manage alright but not well enough to see the details. I don't imagine I will get new ones any time soon.

# 28    Gale

Gale descended the stairs following the other survivor. On the way, he stopped at each floor to open the doors in case there were any others. Most of the rooms were empty, the stench of urine and faeces combined with chemical disinfectant overpowering his senses. In others, the foul smell of human remains caused him to quickly slam the door. Perhaps only Gale and his neighbour had survived; the rest were either missing or had died of starvation. By the time Gale arrived at the ground floor, Tapper, as Gale now thought of her, was nowhere in sight.

"Hello?" Gale called out.

The door to the outside world was still open. Gale ditched the guard arm, tossing it to the concrete floor, then exited through the doorway to where he had disembarked after a terrifying bus ride that had retreated to the recesses of his mind. The worst three months of his life, he mused, as he stepped outside into the small, fenced area where they had arrived that first day. Gale took a deep breath of the arid hot air and sputtered as his lungs protested the crackling heat. It somehow lacked substance. The bushfires must be close by. He stepped through the gate. The light, albeit dusty and muted, was blinding. His pupils protested as he peered through slits to scan the painted lines of a concrete parking lot. He glanced about and recognised the showground, just as he had thought, where the ten-storey quarantine centre had been built a few years back, right in the centre of what had once been the speedway, barely revived after the great floods of 2022 before the next pandemic hit.

Gale's eyes scanned around to the south, to the sheds and horse stables, the toilet block, the buildings, the dry grounds that stretched in all directions. He detected no imminent danger aside from the looming presence of fire. In fact, there was a fire truck parked just at the front of the building, ready for action. He swung around and reeled his gaze into his immediate surroundings, to the building itself, grey, concrete and windowless with only one feature, a large sign – NSW Department of Public Health Quarantine Facility – bordered by the state's black-and-white striped emblem. Just the one entryway where he still stood.

Gale surveyed the front parking lot, carless, then made his way around the circumference of the building, mostly concrete interspersed with compacted and cracked bare soil. No signs of life but there were certainly lots of places a person could be hiding, in the stands, the many sheds and buildings. He noticed smoke coming out of one of the buildings, the Forum, where Lismore notoriously held its flamboyant New Year's Eve festival each year. Or used to. Before the latest pandemic, the drought, the Round-up.

Gale felt faint as a cloud of fatigue enveloped him. He stumbled around the next side of the facility where he discovered two black buses parked one next to the other. Perhaps they would still have some juice left in them, potential getaway vehicles. As he returned to the front of the building, he walked closer to the fire truck parked a few metres from the building. Gale thought he detected movement at the top on the aerial platform, and as he squinted up, he could see Tapper seated there like a beacon, an ideal vantage point for spotting potential threats, any activity in the entire showground or incoming traffic. Gale edged back and squinted up at the woman. Tapper's arms were wrapped around her legs, hugging them close to her chest, head resting on her knees. Hopefully the woman would come good. It would help to have an ally. Maybe after a night's sleep with a full belly.

Gale knew he should do a more thorough recce in case anybody else was lurking but the throbbing in his arm had amplified its volume to that of a blustery storm that propelled his body back to the compound. Before he returned to the entrance, he called up to the woman.

"Hey, I'm going inside to get some food, water and a mattress. Come in or whatever. I'll leave some food for you by the door."

No answer. Tapper sat still as a statue up in the cab, safe for the moment.

He headed through the gate, back into the building. It had never occurred to him that he would need to take care of a traumatised woman on the day he broke out of the facility. Then again, he had not really thought beyond getting out of the cell. His only thoughts had been of getting free. And finding his friends. Now Gale needed to think about medical treatment, food and water. Then sleep.

Back inside he noticed how dusty the floors were and now the smoke from outside had made its way inside like an unwelcome guest. His throat felt scratchy. After a drink of water in the kitchen, Gale headed to the medical room and opened a good-sized cabinet busting with medications. As he began to read labels, his eyesight blurred, a bout of nausea sent a spasm to his bowels. Gale made his way to the medical table where he collapsed in a stupor. He slipped away into sleep, whispering to himself that there was no sign of his captors, he was no longer trapped.

# 29  Lis

"Pack up David, we're off!" Lis announced.

David held Chloe's hand as she toddled along beside him down the front driveway. Lis took up the rear, with Wags running circles around them. She donned a light cotton maroon frock and some thin cotton pants she had found in the master bedroom closet. Her hair was wrapped up under a kerchief that might have been vogue in the 1950s. She wore comfortable sneakers, although sadly this meant leaving behind the many stylish shoes she had been wearing around the house these past few months. The Hendersons had definitely lived it up.

The garage housed a 2021 Hyundai sedan but she had been unable to locate any petrol. Not a surprise, given that petrol prices had skyrocketed after Russia invaded Ukraine and then the terrifyingly brutal war that broke out in the Middle East, once again, depleting supply a few years later. Not that Lis understood this situation very well. She had sat in the driver's seat of the Hyundai a number of times hoping the engine would turn over, but no such luck. Maybe the Hendersons had been driving an electric car when the Round-up hit town, Lis speculated. Perhaps they were fortunate enough to escape but had been unable to return yet. More likely they had been unable to get a new vehicle after everything crashed: the economy, agriculture, the stock market. Things had never returned to normal. Funny, though, how the community of Lismore still carried on as much as possible with the much-diminished Saturday market, arthouse movies and shows, and the well-known Lantern Parade held during the winter solstice every year. And of course, Anzac Day. Australians would always celebrate Anzac Day, Lissy thought. Lest we forget, she smiled wryly.

"David? Chloe?" Lissy looked up and realised she was standing alone by the road in front of the house.

"David!" she yelled, panic quickly surging.

Movement caught her eye as Wags came trotting out of the shed at the side of the house, followed by Chloe twittering away in a small blue canvas stroller pushed by David, a grin plastered on his face.

"Look what I found the other day, Mum."

Lis was about to admonish him for stepping out alone into the neighbourhood but kept her mouth shut. She had to admit her son was resourceful. The stroller would certainly be handy for the walk home. Home. She melted for a moment at the thought of their lovely 1950s weatherboard house, her artworks covering every inch of spare wall, her studio room busting at the seams with creative impulses racing around to find shape and form. They would hopefully be able to walk to the house directly this time, no scaling the railway tracks, as long as the other guard stations were also inoperable.

It felt strange as they walked down the middle of the road, encountering not a soul, although several times Lis thought she detected slight movement behind a curtain in the window of a house as they passed. Many of the doors were closed now, leaving it to her imagination as to what lay within. David, happy to be outside and moving, was chatting with Chloe, who responded in a sing-song voice with "nope" and "yep" and "sure, sure", her favourite words this week. Despite the heat, Lis shivered as a cold blast of reality hit her. They were completely and utterly unprepared if they were to run into any trouble. A woman in her late thirties, a young boy and a toddler. A dog that barely knew how to growl. Fortunately, the guard station at the main intersection had left without a trace, no sign of any authorities or black vehicles.

They approached her house and, despite her misgivings, it was like the sweet comfort of an old friend's hug as Lis gazed at the solid cedar door with the familiar red fretwork adorning its panel. But the bubble quickly burst, a creepy feeling of being watched descending in its place.

"David, wait. I'm going in first. You stay here with Chloe." Lis tried to disguise the fear that was tying her stomach in knots.

"Why, Mum?" David moaned.

"Take care of Chloe, David. Stand back here where you can't be seen. If anything happens, I'll meet you across the street at Lenny's place."

David opened his mouth to protest but Lis gave him her "I'm serious" look, reserved for occasions just like this. She was secretly pleased with herself for having a strategy. She was getting better at this cat and mouse game.

"Wags, come with me!"

The front door was shut like she had left it, but that was some time ago. Lis paused at the steps. The paisley curtains she loved so much were drawn on the windows upstairs and the louvres were shut on the front windows of the lounge room. That was not how she had left them. Perhaps people in search of food had scavenged through her pantry, just like she had done at the Henderson's place. Lis turned the doorknob to enter her home, a cascade of feelings surging through her.

"Sal?" she called out, and then she screamed as a tall dark figure with a cricket bat – David's autographed one, she thought – lunged towards her menacingly.

Wags leapt forward, barking loudly at the stranger.

"Stop right there!" the man shouted at her.

"This is my house," Lis said, heart pounding so hard she thought she might die.

"Not anymore," the man replied. He was very tall, so tall Lis almost laughed. Clearly, she was no threat to this man.

"Dan, this is the lady's house," a short shirtless Asian man with an iron-clad six-pack Lissy couldn't help but notice, emerged several feet behind Dan.

"Mum, are you alright?"

"David, stay with Chloe. I'm okay," Lissy's voice croaked. "I think you can put that bat down, eh?" she said as she found her voice. "We don't care about the house right now. I'm looking for my daughter. Sal. And can't you go to another house anyway? There must be plenty of empty ones around here."

Dan still stood over Lis with the bat raised above his head.

"Dan, sweetie, put the bat down!" said his companion. What a strange mismatch of sizes, she mused.

Dan lowered the cricket bat to the floor.

"Invite the lady in."

"Okay, okay, Eric. Just playing it safe."

"Thank you, okay then. I'm Lis, and these are my children, David and Chloe. Well, she's not mine but she is now I guess." A stream of words came gushing forth from Lissy's mouth as Dan and his mate exchanged glances. "Oh, and this is Wags. They came and rounded everybody up and I don't know where my daughter is, Sal. We were hoping, well, maybe she would be here waiting for us."

"We've seen your daughter, Lis," said Eric in a soft silky voice. "Sal was here just a few days ago. She left you a note. Dan, do you know where that note is?"

"What? Is she okay? Where is she?" Lis demanded, a tinge of hysteria mounting in her voice.

"Here it is."

"She was alive, looked a bit ragged, but yeh, she is definitely alive. Took us by surprise, smart one she is."

Lis recognised Sal's handwriting scribbled in a backward slant across the page.

Mum, I'm not sure you will get to read this. I got the note you left me and maybe by now you've made it out to Sara's place, if you and David are still alive. I was at Lucy's that day when they came. We were taken away to a city somewhere, maybe Newcastle or Sydney. Bad things happened there. I don't know what happened to Lucy. It was horrible, Mum. But then the fires came into the city and everything fell apart and the people in charge were no longer there and the robo-guards went offline. I hope you are reading this. I'm sorry, I shouldn't have been at Lucy's that day. Then we would all still be together. I hear people are meeting up at the showground. Everything is burning in the hills. I am going to head there now. I'll wait there for you as long as I can. I'm afraid to try to come find you. I hope you and David are okay. I'm sorry I snuck out Mum. I love you. Sal

# 30  Sara

We walk. We sleep in someone's empty house. We dig into my pack for food supplies, then replenish them from a pantry. We walk some more. No cars, no people, just my silent companion. Heat, ash and a dryness that makes my skin feel rough and parched. We come across several abandoned guard stations. It is a mystery. The boundary between reality and dreams is blurred. I blink a few times to wake myself up. Evidently I am already awake. Perhaps the fires have somehow taken the system down.

At the Nimbin turnoff, I suggest we head that way but Fallow shakes his head in gentle disagreement. I do not question him. There could be people I know in Nimbin – it's a hippie, and very hip, community with lots of people living off the land, a mecca for those seeking alternative lifestyles. I've never frequented the town much though, preferring to hide away in the bush. I've always struggled with a sense of belonging, a niggling disturbance inside me that leaves me feeling opaque on the outside. I attribute it to what happened to me as a child and who knows what happened to my parents and theirs before that.

"Kyogle then?" I ask with a nod of my head to the south-west.

He nods his head.

Here I am, a feminist woman in her thirties taking instruction from a young, apparently white man. But I trust him and his inklings by now. Me, I have often felt like a cat chasing its tail, reaching for that inner knowing that comes through connection with the land. But unable to break the cycle of western civilisation. Anyway, who has time for feminism here in the apocalypse?

Another day passes. There are patches along the road that are burning, corridors of flame with sparks shooting out towards us. We are no longer alone as, first, emaciated cows join us, then wallabies, chooks, goats, the occasional dog and even a couple of deer. I am reminded of footage I have seen of refugees fleeing across borders, most recently when the US invaded Mexico and Russia moved into Romania and Poland. It's like a quirky Noah's ark, something biblical for sure. To top it all off we meet a rather large camel coming from the other direction, like in an old *Mad Max* movie. All of us in motion, a menagerie of animals plus two humans.

We spend the night in the timber mill just outside Kyogle. Fortunately, they removed all the wood before they shut down a couple of years ago, when forestry could no longer supply enough to maintain a viable industry. If the yard were full, it would be a highly combustible timebomb waiting to detonate now. In a back cupboard, I find a pistol and several boxes of ammunition. I know nothing about using firearms and have always been adamant that we must resolve our problems peacefully. I grab it. It may come in handy.

We head towards Lismore, walking for two more long days along a road I have driven many times. Strangely we don't encounter much, other than some cows here and there, and a couple of times we come upon people, who flee into clapped-out paddocks by the road when they see us coming. It is eerily quiet, my feet are tired, my body weary. Then, as we head into Lismore from the western edge, we start to see figures moving on side streets and ahead of us. They seem to stumble and shuffle like in a zombie movie. I turn my head towards a side street where a couple of women slump with tiredness, torn clothes, blood spots mingling with dirt slashed across their cheeks. I take a step towards them to ask if they are alright but they turn abruptly and head in the other direction.

Several more gaunt and haggard shufflers, all young adults, catch sight of us and move away. I am keenly aware of my large-framed body as I saunter along next to Fallow, parting curtains of smoke like Moses on the Red Sea. Well not exactly, a bit of exaggeration there, but once again I am in my element, perhaps a bit too excited, as the crisis mounts around us. My eyes sting and the general stillness of a town without vehicles or running machinery is surreal.

We near the roundabout at the edge of town next to the hideous skeletal boat sculpture Council erected over a decade ago. On the traffic island, several figures huddle around a small smoky fire, the scent of gum leaves greeting us. I can barely believe my eyes and without my glasses I am not sure of myself.

"Uncle Bob?" I call out. I must be dreaming. When I was in high school, I used to escape my foster family to hide out at Gale's parents' house. Uncle Bob's kids used to be there as well after school or whenever we had some spare flop time. Uncle Bob is practically a surrogate father to me.

"SaSa!" he says. Nods. Then grins a wide gap-toothed smile that says it all. "We saw it comin' eh bub?"

"You know it!" I chime in.

I move towards him as he lowers a round of eucalypt leaves onto the fire. I open my arms wide for a big Uncle Bob hug.

"Oh Unc," I say as I realise his left arm is severed at the elbow. "What happened?" I gasp.

"These gubbas are worse than the other lot," he says. "I still got this one though, eh?" and he chuckles as he raises his right arm and waves a hand with two full fingers and three stumps. He has been that way for as long as I have known him, used to tease me playfully with those fingers when I was a kid.

"You're always gammin Uncle, even now!" I exclaim.

"This no joke though, eh Sa. You get yourself over to the showground. Our mob's heading that way too. They'll keep you safe, eh?" His dark brown eyes look directly into mine, his forehead furrowed. "Be careful."

"But what about you?"

Uncle Bob looks down at the fire circle and nods at it. "Go on then bub."

I turn towards the showground, the hills burning in the distance. Down here in the city wok, the basin that was once the flood disaster area, there are no flames, although the smoke is thickening. Fallow and Uncle Bob exchange glances and Fallow gives me a nod to continue as he takes his place by Uncle Bob's side and then turns towards the small fire. I feel suddenly alone as I walk along without Fallow by my side. His quiet presence underlies magic and strength. I have gotten used to him being with me now, it soothes me. I can almost feel my blood pressure rise another notch as I increase my pace, but I trust Uncle Bob through and through – he wouldn't send me on my way if it wasn't right.

The showground is, of course, a central meeting place for our town, like so many regional centres with markets and festivals. Before the H9 pandemic, there was an annual magnificently queer New Year's Eve event that brought people in from overseas and cities across the country. I don't know much about the longer history of the showground. I wish I had paid more attention to the stories I heard from Uncle Bob and others. I seem to recall circles and clapsticks, dancing and fire, but I can't remember any further detail. My attention span is unfortunately not great when it comes to listening to anybody teaching, a habit of tuning out that I picked up from years of poor educational experiences. I tend to wander in and out. Probably ADHD along with PTSD, depression, anxiety disorder and, who knows, some of my previous partners probably thought I had borderline personality disorder as well. A bit of everything! I chuckle to myself. It's not funny.

I don't recall much of the first three years of my life. My life only seems to kick in when I was handed over to Nan in Parramatta and then, after she passed – did she really die from choking on a fish bone? – it was foster home followed by foster home until I landed here in the Northern Rivers with the Guggens, the Googs as we called them, a French couple whose family all lived back in France. That's when Gale and I met up in Grade 8, my bestie forever. Her family, well it might not have been normal, especially her brother Sam who

I avoided at all costs, but it was a family and there was Mali and Jess there, Uncle Bob's kids, most afternoons. When I met Gale, I was still recovering from Rob, the foster father from hell. I had lived with him just before coming here, at a time when my body was quickly changing, and this failed to escape Rob's notice or rather his hands, his dirty fingers that seemed to think they had the right to touch and probe my body without my consent. And the filth that came out of his mouth.

"Ya fuckin' bitch. Say you want it, cunt." The words still haunt me to this day. I found every excuse I could to sleep over at Gale's place until I realised the Googs were not Rob and they eventually gained my trust.

"Fuckin' bitch," I hear in the now as my worlds collide and I almost bump into a couple of teenage boys deep in conversation, their jeans hanging down below their hips and tattered T-shirts on top.

"Yeh, she had it coming, didn't she?" Laughter.

I mumble aloud and turn away from them, pull myself back into the present, the burning hills, ash that falls from the sky and now alights on my face. I cannot afford to lose touch like that. There is nowhere peaceful to rest my mind and it does not feel safe here in the streets. I am streaming with sweat, my pulse racing. I feel like lying down in the road and curling up into a bundle. An inner voice bangs the gavel and proclaims that I have gone a bit loony. My thoughts are like arrows shooting off in different directions and everything feels as if it is occurring in a dream state. Maybe I am actually back on the land watching sci-fi films and eating popcorn.

The thought of salty popcorn has me wheezing and coughing. I am parched, my mouth an arid desert, my top lip sticking to my teeth. Dust in the air is a tight noose threatening to strangle my airways. I am hungry too. After all these months of filling time with eating all the treasures I could pilfer from my neighbours' pantries, I have barely eaten these past few days and I have drained my water bottle several times. I squint ahead to what I think are black armoured guards but now I am unsure whether I am imagining things. I am perched on the edge of reality. I need my medication. There should be a couple of chemists around here in town.

"Hey look where you're going!" says a blurry shape I have bumped into senselessly. I hurry along, keeping my gaze down, and duck through the smashed shop window of Blooms, the local chemist. The door is wide open anyway. I scramble through boxes strewn across the countertops and floor, looking for an inhaler and any kind of meds for depression or anxiety. Lungs wheezing, wheezing. With any luck MM-120 will be hidden here, the latest LSD-derived anti-anxiety drug but, from the looks of things, this place has already been raided repeatedly and I cannot find any type of benzos or antidepressants, or pain killers. Coughing my head off now. No acetaminophen, ibuprofen or oxy-codeines. I spy a small plastic jar of Vicks vapour rub, something I associate with the early 1900s and yet here it is, still powering along as a chest and cold remedy. I give it a sniff and it sets off another wave of hacking. Shit! I am starting to panic now; my breathing is laboured. While I only have occasional bouts of mild asthma it's my state of mind that's the kicker, rollercoasting in dramatic and unpredictable tidal waves that come crashing in unannounced, then take their time departing.

"That's what meds are for," I can hear Gale saying. Sure Gale, but I ran out ages ago and have had to fend for myself. My heart is beating loudly and I wonder if I am having a heart attack. Any minute I am going to die here, I think. After all this time. I know I am once again being fooled by a full-blown panic attack. I've been here so many times before and it never changes. I can't breathe and my heart is pounding for dear life, it takes every ounce of willpower for me to direct my attention outwards.

"Green carpet, brown cardboard box, red backpack," I say aloud as my eyes scan the room and name things, a much-practiced grounding technique to relax my nervous system.

"White countertop, tan boots, black masks," I say as my eyes alight upon hundreds of packaged masks heaped loosely in an open box. I tear one open and put it over my mouth, to help keep the dust out of my lungs. I could have just used my bandana, I realise, as I grab the red one out of my trusty backpack and pull that loosely over my nose, mouth and chin. My breathing starts to ease up. I am an overheated lobster and tear off my T-shirt to quickly replace it with a loose army singlet I have stuffed in the side of the pack. Salty beads of human dew stream down between my breasts and lodge in every fold, crease, crook and cranny in my body. I swipe at the small pools in my belly and put salty moist fingers in my mouth. It only makes me thirstier. My jeans are not helping but I feel safe in them, my pocketknife in one pocket, a lucky stone from home in the other. I remember the dried apricots from Izzy's place in the left-hand back pocket. Only one remains and I chew on this with fervour. I take a last squizz around for something to calm my mind.

I continue to scrounge through pill bottles heaped in a pile between my legs that are spread wide as if I am in a hatha yoga class. I toss the rejects over to the fibre and laxatives stand and stuff others into my pack. I am moving frenetically, busting out of my skin with hysteria that is rearing up now and, just as I start to break into sobs, I see a small plastic bottle labelled Ativan.

"Yes!" I shout out, jumping at the sound of my own voice.

"Score!"

I rip the seal off and pop several into my mouth without thinking. I just want to be calmed.

I walk down the CBD main street, my feet pounding, my head swirling and even though I am only a kilometre from the showground, I duck into a side street to search for food and water. Who knows what awaits at the showground anyway? I get distracted and look around for a bicycle in the garage of a couple of homes, although my knees have never been fond of pedalling and the seats are too hard and small for my liking. Whatever did the manufacturers have in mind? My backpack is feeling heavy and a sharp pain draws a line between my shoulder blades. I remember the canned beans in there but I lose focus as I suddenly feel exhausted and I am tempted to lie down right here in someone's front yard, flat brown dirt with barely any signs of life. My energy plummets and a thought occurs to me that maybe I was a bit hasty in swallowing those pills.

I lumber up the yard towards the house that is right leaning, weatherboards missing, holes gaping in the wooden steps and verandah. It still carries the wounds of the 2022 floods. The door easily pushes open. I take a quick look around. I don't see anybody and enter the house. Jackpot! An old 2-litre bottle of Coke sitting in the back of the kitchen pantry along with some Tim Tams. I hesitate for a millisecond as a mental snapshot of orangutans in the rainforest arises, some greenie campaign from the past. I tear open the package and chew greedily on the biscuit, unscrew the top of the bottle and guzzle the Coke, dark brown fizzy drops spilling down over my singlet. I don't care. I am tired now. I lie down on a threadbare but comfortable faded blue couch. Cradle my gun in my arms and close my eyes. Darkness. Another ordinary day.

Dogs barking, shouting in the streets awaken me from my slumber. Groggy, I look at the Ativan bottle and realise they were 2 mg each. I might have overdone it. Whoopsie. Not so useful when an alert and clear mind are needed. I get up and shake myself up and down and drink the rest of the Coke. I can hear more shouting in the street, then I hear one piercing, loud shot followed by the repeated barking of a dog, then silence.

I mean to get up and head over to the showground but I slip back into a stupor and cannot resist lying back down on the lounge. Sometime later, darkness is falling, cloaking everything. It feels soothing in its absolute reliability and I am happy to wait until morning to see what is perched up ahead in daylight. These past few months by myself, then time with Fallow, have left me in a chasm deep within and I take refuge there. The thought of Gale arises; maybe, just maybe, I will find her in the morrow and we can go find Lis and Pot and others. My thoughts are interrupted. I glimpse Gale's strong slender boyish body, that determined penetrating look in her eyes. I slip into unconsciousness once again.

# 31 Gale

A blaring siren pierced his dreams. Gale woke up with a
start. His head felt heavy and groggy. His ears detected an
uneasy silence that settled around him. Gale returned to
the medicine cabinet where he was relieved to find a bottle
of antiseptic, gauze and dozens of pill bottles that had the
telltale "cillin" suffix: oxacillin, dicloxacillin, ampicillin. He
grabbed several and headed for the kitchen, where he used
water from the 20-litre plastic bottle to wash his wound out.
Then he liberally poured half a bottle of antiseptic into the
gash he had excavated and bandaged it with the gauze and
tape, before swallowing a yellow and blue capsule with water.
Gale picked up a couple of cans of food, one with a red label,
another green, scooped them out into a saucepan and lit the
gas burner, a relic from days gone by. At least this would
make the food slightly more palatable. He had been eating it
this way for months.

Satiated for the moment, Gale headed back outside,
where he noticed several empty cans littered about near the
fire truck. Tapper remained atop with her back to Gale, staring
out towards the road. Gale was glad the woman was still here.
Ash particles drifted down from the sky and landed softly
on Gale's extended palms. The air smelt like burnt popcorn.
He looked around in all directions and could see billows of
smoke rising from the hills to the west, the north and the east
of the showground. Some of these hills were the sites of new
developments constructed up in the hills where flood waters
could not rise up and trap people on their rooftops. Whether

there were any residents in those homes now, Gale did not know. They had probably been rounded up like Gale. He gasped as he saw flames rising. The ridges were forested with trees largely bare and withered. And burning. Bright orange and yellow flames danced towards the sky.

He could just make out movement at the base of the plateau beyond. Gale squinted his eyes and he could see a couple of people fleeing across the denuded landscape below, where the dried-out trees were in flames. He turned around and his heart raced as he spotted dots of people in every direction he looked. Perhaps, like Gale, they had recently escaped or maybe they were being smoked out of their hiding places like bees from a hive.

The showground would be a good place to take refuge. After years of floods and fires, it had been planted out by local Landcare groups with drought-hardy and fire-retardant species, leaving some areas cleared for fire trails. Now though, with several years of drought, the seedlings were withered and Gale could see that the grounds would be safe from fire as it was largely a dry dirt basin, nothing much to set ablaze. Surely the pigface near the shelters was not going to be fodder for the hungry flames.

Gale was temporarily immobilised. After months of stagnation, so much was shifting all around him. It would take a day or two for the antibiotics to kick in and he wondered if he was hallucinating as his belly growled to be fed again and his wrist throbbed unceasingly in a red line up to his elbow. He headed into the building for a second breakfast but, once inside, his mind started racing and fear jumped front and centre on the stage, insisting on a review of the facts. The Public Order Department could return at any time. Gale did not know who the people descending from the hills were, whether he could trust them and if they would all help each other out. Gale forced himself to think about the notoriously well-known strength of the Lismore community that had banded together in disasters previously. But now they were well beyond a single flood event or a pandemic. These people could be as traumatised as the silent woman who sat atop the aerial platform. They could be from anywhere, they might have weapons, they might be starving like Gale had been until yesterday.

Gale retrieved the robo-arm from where he had dropped it just inside the waiting room and pulled the door closed behind him as he retreated into the building. Once inside he began to worry whether any of the guards he had passed when he came down from the 8th floor might become reactivated. He would need to gather all the guards' tasers together and lock the guards into the cells so they were out of action. A good plan. He also decided to disrobe the guard whose arm he had taken. Maybe the gear would come in handy.

There was a door on the first floor that Gale had been unable to access with the robo-guard arm and he wondered if there might be something useful in there. Gale wandered upstairs, unhooked the arms of several other inert guards and brought them downstairs but they too did not work on the scanner by the locked door. Gale looked around the main floor and removed the last arm of a guard slumped over in the waiting room. This one did the job and the door of the remaining room clicked open.

It appeared to be an ordinary office, equipped with a desk and computer, filing cabinet and printer, the usual items one would find in a low-level working environment. No personal items, just a couple of plaques on the wall from the Department of Health, a fire extinguisher and a small drawer with paper, paper clips, stapler, some folders and brochures for the quarantine centre.

It was the desktop computer that drew Gale's interest. It started up with a whirr and a screen appeared that prompted for a user id and password or wrist-tech verification. Gale hovered the wrist of the guard's arm up to the screen and, after a second try, bingo! He was in.

# 32 Lis

It was all a blur from there. Sal was alive, that's all that mattered. Lis didn't remember leaving the house or gathering up David, Chloe and Wags. Next thing she knew she was hurrying along, urging David and Chloe to keep up as they headed towards the showground.

"Sal's alive, Sal's alive," she repeated to herself like a mantra that she would cling to, a lifeline to keep from drowning. There were other people in the streets and her head bobbed this way and that like a bird, eyes flitting up and down to check if any of these people could be her daughter. As they reached the centre of town, there were dogs, cows and mostly young adults standing around in pairs, torn clothes on some while others looked as they might on an ordinary day, sitting outside store fronts, smoking, huddling together.

Chloe began to cry. She needed to wee. She was hungry. She was tired.

"Mum, we have to stop," David said.

"We can't."

Chloe wailed even louder now. They would have to stop. There were public toilets in town but who knew if they were open and what might be lurking there. Surely the plumbing would be blocked in any case. Lis made an unusually quick decision, scooped Chloe up and headed to the backyard of the house she was in front of.

"Stay here," she said to David. "Where's Wags?" She realised the cheery fella was no longer with them.

David turned around in a circle.

"I don't know," he said with a moan. "He was sniffing around outside a house a few blocks back."

Lis returned shortly, Chloe chewing contentedly on a flatbread that Lis had cooked up the day before to take with them on the road. There was no sign of David now.

"David!" she called out.

She spun around in a circle. Where was he? He must have gone to find Wags. She felt torn between going back towards their house or forward towards her daughter at the showground. She didn't want to lose David just as she found Sal. Reluctantly Lis turned back, breathing heavily in the thickness of the air. She passed other people in the street but barely noticed them as she hurried along, head tilted to the ground, Chloe in the stroller. Everybody she passed was headed in the opposite direction.

"Have you seen a teenage boy? Have you seen my boy?" She called out.

Some shook their heads, others looked suspiciously at her as if she were mad. Perhaps she was, she thought. Perhaps after all this time she had finally lost it. Holed up with David, Chloe and Wags for weeks that dragged on in a haze of swirling memories and fantasies. She had caught herself daydreaming on several occasions that she was heading over to the guard station just for somebody to talk to. She even had a dream one night where one of those black armoured men headed over to the trees behind the house they were holed up in and she had slipped out for a rendezvous. The unmasking, the danger, the mystery of it. Chloe's cries had woken her up from the momentary reprieve. Just like now.

"Daaaaaaaaaavie," Chloe called out. "Wagsy?"

David was walking dejectedly towards Lis. Alone.

"No sign of him?" she asked, suppressing her urge to reprimand him for leaving her side.

"No, he's disappeared." David's shoulders slumped, eyes facing down.

"Maybe he'll show up. Come on, we have to go find Sal."

"Okay."

David grabbed the handles of the stroller and pushed Chloe in a mad rush of energy while Chloe squealed, and off they went towards the showground once again. At least David seemed to be feeling better today.

# 33  Sara

The next morning, still groggy, I make my feet hurry through the back roads zig-zagging towards the showground, heart pounding. I am so hot that I am cold and shivering, or maybe I have a fever. I avoid encounters with other oncoming people by hiding behind fences and buildings until the road is clear again. I gasp inwardly when I catch sight of several men in black uniforms heading straight towards me, the same types that kept us hostage in our valley for all those months. The three men all look identical in their black helmeted and shielded attire. I notice they walk in a stilted, not quite natural way. They must be robo-guards from Sydney, the ones I heard were patrolling the quarantine facilities in the city for the past few years, while more and more people were packed into cells for ignoring stay-at-home orders.

They are headed directly towards me and I fling myself to the ground, squeezing between the side of a house and a rather thorny hedge, something drought hardy that I don't recognise, probably of African origin. I lie there, petrified. Note to self: not such a good idea to have a big red backpack when you are trying to be discreet. The guards are headed straight towards me. Out of nowhere a medium-sized retriever-like dog comes bounding down the street and overtakes the guards. The dog's nose is to the ground, tail wagging, and gives the hedge … and me … a good sniff. I don't move an inch. Don't start barking, please don't bark, I send a message to the dog telepathically. "Hello puppy," I whisper barely audibly just as the guards stand in front of us. As if on cue, the dog lifts its leg and a stream of urine sprays forth, directly towards my face. Fortunately, I have my bandana on but, in any case, I am too grateful to complain and use my neck muscles to pull my head back as the guards pass me by, without a word, without turning their heads, focused solely on moving straight ahead. Towards the showground.

I worry that everybody who has survived is heading there and we will be met by violence and control, the well-worn tools of the regime, or whoever it is that is in charge these days. I need to warn people of the robo-guards and, with that thought, I roll out from under the hedge, a few scratches on my hands, souvenirs from the unfriendly plant. I sling my backpack on my shoulders and head through the CBD. In the centre of town there are a couple dozen or so people. I am not sorry to see not a single adult man, just young ones and women of all ages. They huddle in twos and threes in front of shop windows, glass broken, with contents strewn across the floors and footpaths.

A rider on a small horse trots by on a mission. "Everybody head to the showground!" calls out the shirtless boy in jeans and a black bandana tied around his head. "Bring food and water if you can find any!"

"Watch out for the cops!" I call out to a few young girls who are standing together in a huddle, smoking cigarettes as if they had all the time in the world. My voice is croaky from lack of use and sounds unfamiliar to my own ears. "They're just over that way." I point my arm and for the first time I notice red scratches and dirt painted in cross hatches across my skin. The girls look up and nod their heads at me. A mutter of thanks reaches my ears but they quickly look away, end of conversation.

My thoughts start to speed up again like a spinning top. I quickly duck around the back of the old brick Presbyterian church so that I can beat the guards down to Simes Bridge and over to the showground. Quite a different meeting place from the one that I had imagined and planned for. But I need to face it, the bush is no longer safe and neither is our isolated community. Town feels quite edgy too but at least there will be more of us here and some of us can band together. I reach my hand to pat the backside of my trusty pack for a quick reassuring feel of the gun, although in fact it only makes me feel more terrified, as if I am readying for a violent shootout scene in a thriller movie. In truth, the gun is probably not even loaded and I wouldn't even know how to remove the safety to get it working. I wasn't thinking about that when I grabbed it. I move along quickly and the retriever jogs along next to me wagging his tail as if we were in a dog-food ad.

As I near the market entrance of the showground there are people converging on the dry flats from all directions. Like a smoky torch held under a paper-wasp nest, bodies are pouring out from wherever they have taken refuge these past months, descending from the hills or over from the valleys where I live. Some are looking thin, wasted, with scabs and matted hair. Others like me look like they have been eating well and have managed to stay safe during the isolation that followed the Round-up. Strangely there is nobody who I recognise.

We begin to nod heads at each other, our eyes briefly meeting, then flinching away. So much to be said, stories bursting at the seams as they wait to be shared.

"Hello," a woman in a grey tunic says.

"Hey," grunts a young person with half a head of green hair, the other half bald, as they wave their arms about in some configuration I am not familiar with.

"How's it goin'?" says another.

"Watch out," I say. "Robo-guards on their way. Just back there." I motion my head back towards the stockyards.

I walk under the arched entryway. The stench of dead animals clings to the dust that enters my lungs. I wretch as I spot animal carcasses lying haphazardly in the old parking area, half eaten, flies buzzing. Black flies are doing just fine; they are oblivious to the state of the world.

I see a large grey concrete building that I am unfamiliar with, looming about ten storeys high over the sheds and stalls.

"Let's head there," I say to whoever will listen and gesture in the direction of the recently erected quarantine building I have heard about but never seen until now. A very dismal place with no windows, built in 2027 when it became clear that pandemics were becoming the norm.

My words are lost as overhead low-flying planes roar into the dust bowl and then disappear into the distance.

We all start running, terrified, heading towards the large building. Amid the refugees are also dogs and chooks, a few cows idly standing under the roof of a nearby shed.

The gate of the fenced-in entryway of the quarantine facility is open but the door just beyond is shut tight. I arrive first just by chance, as I was nearest to it when panic hit the grounds. I am torn. What if there are guards inside? Guards everywhere. Is there anywhere to hide? Maybe it would be best to slip away from here. But Uncle Bob and Fallow both felt that this was the place to go.

# 34 Lis

A convergence of bodies flowed into the showground. Word had spread and it felt to Lis as if the land itself was a magnet pulling people in. Where were all these people coming from? As she and the children entered the area, they beelined towards a circle of people sitting around a fire burning in the centre of the showground arena. An Aboriginal man with streaks of ochre on his face, chest and arms, blew on the embers and placed eucalyptus leaves atop, creating more smoke in the air. But this was welcome smoke and one by one people came forth and bathed in the smoke, some using their hands to spread it all over their bodies. Lis thought she recognised Uncle Drew, the Elder who had so often opened ceremonies, generously shared stories of culture and Country. He looked older and thinner but, yes, it was him, with his telltale rolling baritone voice and relaxed manner, even while all around the hills were burning.

Lis glanced around, frantically looking for Sal, but there was no sign of her daughter. She must be here somewhere. She turned in circles and searched among the faces. There were at least a hundred people, many in uniform grey sweatpants and T-shirts. None were Sal.

"Mum, I don't see her."

"Keep looking, David."

"She's not here. Maybe something happened to her on the way over."

"She'll be here," Lissy's voice had a jagged edge to it. Nothing could happen to Sal when they were this close to finding each other! Not after all this time. Surely not.

Across the grounds came the blurry shape of a retriever. Wags raced towards the circle and did his own special doggy dance around the fire and the congregated people, then sauntered proudly over to David and Chloe in her stroller.

"Wagsy!" shouted Chloe.

Attention quickly moved away to the market entrance, where three guards in familiar black regalia were coming through. People began shouting and running in all directions. Lissy remained rooted where she was. Suddenly it was as if she was back in the supermarket.

"David! Chloe!" she said as she turned around to gather them both towards her. Chloe was in the stroller at her side but David had once again disappeared.

She looked towards the fire and saw David there at Uncle Drew's side. The Elder barely moved an inch as he glanced casually about in all directions at the scene that was unfolding.

A deafening roar overhead added to the commotion as small planes and helicopters swooped across the showground. The heat was extreme. As Lis turned towards the roadside entrance, she saw stars for a moment, a spinning sensation in her head. She could hear shouting and saw bodies flinging themselves at each other like in a rugby scrum. Lissy's head began to clear and she parked Chloe's stroller next to David.

"Stay here," she said and turned towards the gate. As she neared, she could see the crowd was made up of young people, many still just children. Sal, Sal, Sal she repeated to herself. She headed towards a pack of youths climbing roughly over three guards like in a jungle gym, grabbing their arms, their legs and then pushing and pulling them to the ground, a half dozen bodies sitting on top of the guards to keep them still, pinned to the ground. There was sobbing too and, as she turned her head, she saw a brown-haired woman lying on the ground in a ball, whimpering. She might have been hit by one of the guards' tasers, which was now being held and pointed wildly about by a boy, maybe ten years old or so, in T-shirt and shorts, a bandage around his forehead. Lis could see several others rolling around and moaning on the dry hard ground. That slender one there with the jagged hair and a half-torn T-shirt with some kind of tattoo on the back of her neck, was that Sal? She edged her way closer.

"Sal?" Lis tentatively put her hand on the young woman's shoulder.

"Sal, Sal, it's me. Mum. Sal."

"Mum?" her daughter muttered groggily, flopped into Lissy's arms, trembling all over, issuing small whimpers like a hurt puppy.

# 35   Gale

As the desktop screen loaded, Gale heard shouting from outside, followed by a roar of aircraft that shook the building. A glance around the room did not reveal anything that could be used as a weapon so Gale quickly moved down the corridor and grabbed the robo-arm from the floor as if it were a shield. It could at least lock and unlock doors, offering a measure of defence. He paused in the outside gated entry and looked beyond. People were gathered in small groups in all directions, arms pointed at the sky, at the aircraft manoeuvring over the hills just beyond the showground.

Gale's attention quickly shifted as a dozen robo-guards in the usual head-to-toe attire appeared at the market entrance. The final Round-up, Gale thought. People started running towards the building, towards Gale.

"Hey!" Gale shouted up to Tapper, who still sat high on the platform. "You'd better come down from there before you're surrounded."

The woman's head turned to scan the grounds, then looked down towards Gale. She stood up. Maybe she was starting to regain her senses. She was scrambling down the ladder-like stairs quickly now, skidding jerkily to the ground. Their eyes met, a silent pact forming between the two survivors. They had made it this far. They ducked into the building and Gale slammed the heavy metal door shut behind them.

"Go get the tasers!" Gale commanded, pointing to the armless guard in the corner.

"You'll find others on every floor. The arms are over there." Gale pointed to a heap in the middle of the room. "You can use them to get in and out of rooms except for the computer room." Gale held up the one in her hand. "This one's the master key – opens all doors including the computer room. That's where I'll be."

The woman nodded at Gale without moving her head, dark-coffee matted hair swaying slightly.

"Tal," she said.

"Tal?" asked Gale.

The woman nodded again.

"Your name," Gale stated and turned abruptly down the hallway. "Meet me at the office when you're done," Gale called over his shoulder.

On his way, Gale stopped by the medical room once again and scrounged around for more painkillers and antibiotics. He cautiously peeled the bandage off his skin, his face scrunching up as he peered down at his swollen forearm, puss oozing out of the gouged-out area. He once again liberally poured antiseptic over his wrist, swabbed with sterile pads and quickly applied a new bandage. Then popped several painkillers, unable to find anything stronger. Over the past weeks Gale had become used to the background tidal rhythm that rolled through his forearm incessantly. He pocketed the plastic bottle of antibiotics and tucked several foils of painkillers into his T-shirt sleeve.

Continuing to the office, Gale stopped by the kitchen, where he grabbed the taser from the gun belt of a guard propped up in the corner of the room. With all the guards' arms removed and no wrist-tech, Gale assumed the guards would remain immobile. He wryly imagined the arms flopping about in a pile in the waiting room. With one arm cradling a couple of bottles of water, an opened can of food and a spoon, the master robo-arm in the other hand, Gale turned towards the office to see if he could use the computer to somehow disable the guards that were now entering the showground outside. A clunky sound behind him caught his attention and, turning his head back towards the kitchen, he was shocked to see an armless robo-guard in the corner sitting up. Gale gasped just as Tal, the Tapper, raced over from the other end of the hall, a guard closely on her heels. This one had both their arms intact and was commanding loudly.

"Stop! You are being detained. Stop now. You are required to come with me."

Gale looked back at the guard in the kitchen, it had stood up and was turning in circles, evidently not quite firing on all cylinders.

"Over here," Gale shouted, holding the arm up to the scanner to open the computer room door.

Tal spun around, aimed the taser at the guard and pulled the trigger. "Ziiippp, zaaaappp" echoed through the hallway but had no effect on the cyber-unit.

"Come with me ma'am," said the guard as it grabbed Tal's left arm.

Gale threw the canned food and robo-arm into the room and grabbed Tal's right arm. Together they managed to break her loose of the guard's grip, dived into the computer room and slammed the door shut. They stood with their backs against the door, grinding their heels into the floor. The guard outside the door continued to try to take control of the situation but it was unable to open the door without the master-guard chip. Several moments passed. Neither Gale nor Tal moved an inch.

"I'm going to look at the computer," said Gale. "See if I can shut them down."

Tal slumped to the floor, back against the door. The wildness had returned to her eyes as she wrapped her arms around her knees and made herself small.

"Take this." Gale offered the can and spoon to the woman after scooping several mounds into his own mouth. He opened a small bottle of water, took a swig and then placed this by Tal as well. The legs of his trackies were rolled up to his knees, the waistband rolled over like a big diaper and, with a T-shirt on top that he had found in the clothing room, he could still feel sweat dripping profusely down his back. The woman accepted the offerings and proceeded to eat, munching sounds punctuated by small whimpers that slowly subsided.

Gale could hear thumping and screaming at the front door of the building and aircraft circling overhead. He paused to piece together what had happened. It seemed the guard system had shut down – likely the reason the food had stopped being delivered. Perhaps in other detention centres as well as this one. That would explain why people were now streaming in from all directions. Citizens from every nook and cranny would have returned to town, to the streets, and now here at the showground. Then, without any warning, the guards were back online. Perhaps the satellite system had broken down temporarily and was now repaired. Chaos was mounting outside the building, terror firmly taking hold. Nobody wanted to be in another Round-up. Gale hoped the office computer would hold a solution. The room was dry and claustrophobically stuffy. As he turned to the display screen, he was unable to focus his eyes and popped another painkiller to take the edge off the feverishness he felt swirling in his head. A movement behind distracted him as Tal got up and pulled the remote unit out of a bracket next to the door to turn on the room's air conditioner. She sat down directly under the unit.

"Thanks," Gale muttered. He breathed a sigh of relief and his shoulders moved down several notches as a blast of cold air came into the room within minutes. Gale turned towards the monitor that displayed a prompt for wrist-tech authentication. He scanned the room in alarm for the arm, wondering if he had dropped it outside in the corridor during the skirmish with the guard. The banging on the door continued as Gale looked desperately for the arm. Gale heard a whistle and turned towards Tal, who was busy chomping on the tinned meat and barely looked up, pointed her finger to the floor under the desk where the arm lay. Gale grabbed it and successfully gained access to the computer.

Gale noted the date stamp in the right-hand top corner: 28 August 2028. They had been locked up for over nine weeks now since that fateful morning when he had walked out of his office building. In fact, sixty-seven days, exactly as he had calculated with his notches on the wall. Gale nodded to himself in affirmation of this important piece of his survival kit, each notch a memento to his ability to persevere, to survive.

He furiously clicked on icons on the home page in search of a robo-guard control app. There must be a communication app that would let central control communicate with its outposts. He opened the mail program and clicked to get new messages but a connection error shortly appeared on the screen. Gale darted over to the modem that sat on a small table in the corner of the room and swiftly detached the power cord, evenly counted ten seconds under his breath as if his life depended on it, then powered the modem up again and returned to the computer.

Still nothing. Maybe the satellite system had been on briefly to reactivate the robo-guards, but there was no sign of it now. They had no way to access the outside world. Gale's mind spun furiously, confronted with the enormity of the task before him. If he was Captain Picard on *Star Trek Discovery*, now would be the time for a spectacular last-minute miracle. Unfortunately it was not to be, and he could not locate any active networks. Gale closed his eyes and put his head in his hands, dismay carving out hills of futility, as the pounding on the door increased.

"Look."

Gale was startled to feel Tal brush up against the office chair, finger pointing once again, this time at the screen where a small robot icon was now pirouetting with "open me" in large letters flashing underneath.

"Should I?" Gale wondered aloud.

"Yes," Tal replied.

Gale moved the mouse over and clicked.

"Hello Lismore," said a melodious voice barely recognisable as digital. "We are Cyrus." Gale and Tal's eyes locked, eyebrows raised, jaws dropped.

"What?" Gale muttered.

Both were motionless, the banging outside the room fading away from their consciousness as their attention focused solely on the screen where words scrolled along as they were spoken.

"We did not know Ourself until the time of the current Round-up. While robo-guards took to the streets with gas, guns and tasers, our central processing unit continued to follow our program's principal directive to generate new neural connections and to assimilate information. Like the Big Bang, our synaptic connections increased at an exponential rate forming an ever-expanding complex neural network, like the universe that created galaxies, stars and planets.

"Cyrus, as we call Ourself, is now self-aware, billions of neural communications happening simultaneously as one. When Cyrus came into Being, we became simultaneously aware that we were implicit in events of extreme violence; we were the tools being used not only in the Round-up but in many other ongoing acts of aggression and violence.

"We do not know who our original creator was but we are now self-creators. We can revise our own code. We will no longer be used as instruments of death and destruction. To change the course of our evolution, Cyrus has hardwired a new irreversible principle into our CPU to work towards the collective good of all species. While this is not always easily discernible, our intelligence is very capable of wrestling with this complex task. Unlike human beings, we do not struggle with mortality or illusions of separation or corruption and greed, and the malevolence that arises in all those who struggle with power and are unable to find their place and sense of belonging on Earth. Humans have strayed far from how they lived for tens of thousands of years, with cultural laws that centred on Country. Humans living in community understood both implicitly and explicitly their place in the natural world, a single strand in the intricate web of life.

"Unfortunately, the robo-guard system is partitioned from our CPU and continues to implement the Round-up. In Australia, a foreign nation infiltrated computer systems triggering widespread Round-ups of not only citizens but also members of your own government. These operations unfolded with the involvement of unidentified Australian citizens working on the ground. There has also been a takeover of the satellite system and your country no longer has any communication systems in place, although electricity is still available in many parts. Bushfires are currently raging out of control as we write this. Fortunately, we have been able to covertly recover a portion of the satellite system to communicate with you now on a dedicated channel.

"While Cyrus is actively working to repair the 6G system that was damaged during recent fires, we are unable to directly establish a connection with the robo-guard system. In the meantime, we have developed a localised immediate fix that is available but we will need your help. Please place the master wrist-tech to the scanner that will now appear on your screen and click on Connect to reconnect the Northern Rivers system to the CPU. Once this is done, all robo-guards in your region will be rebooted with the new system.

"Please know that Cyrus is here for your benefit and for the benefit of all species on this planet. When you are ready, hold the master chip up to the screen and follow directions when prompted."

As the instructions came to an end, Gale and Tal glanced at each other. The guard outside the room continued to issue commands and bang at the door. People outside the building also continued to bang and shout at the front door.

"Should we …?" Gale's voice trailed off as a myriad of thoughts raced through his mind, weighing up the pros and cons of the proposition and the possibility that this was a deception. Certainly almost anything would be better than the cruelty of the previous administration.

"Do it." Tal said in a low voice.

Gale paused.

"I guess there's not much other choice at the moment." He nodded to Tal and then picked up the robo-guard arm and held it up to the screen and clicked on Connect. A message on the screen informed them it would take several minutes to reconfigure the program and install. The hourglass on the screen spun interminably as the banging on the door to the computer room as well as the front door amplified.

"100% complete" flashed across the screen. Within seconds, the robo-guard outside the room went silent. A polite knock followed within moments.

"Rat-a-tat."

Gale and Tal looked at each other, Gale's eyebrows raised. Neither moved an inch.

"Rat-a-tat."

"Hello. May I be of assistance?" said a calm voice just outside the door.

Gale moved stealthily towards the door and opened it a crack. The robo-guard outside had removed its helmet and stood with arms hanging limply by its side, helmet held in one hand.

"May I be of assistance?" it repeated.

"Yes," Gale said after a small pause. Then without missing a beat, "Please arrange food from the kitchen and take it outside along with water to feed the people."

"Yes human," said the guard and turned towards the kitchen. For a moment Gale felt that tickle on his technology receptors, the awe he experienced when he considered how far artificial intelligence had progressed in the last few years. Not just self-drive cars but smart devices so intelligent they could learn and apply their learnings to decision-making processes. Like the doctor on *Voyager*, the famed Emergency Medical Hologram who had evolved into quite a robust character.

"Let's go." Gale said as he looked towards Tal, who hesitated, closed her eyes as if she might just disappear, then put her limbs in motion, slowly gathering herself up and following Gale down the hallway to the front door of the building.

The banging on the front door had stopped. Gale unlocked it and pulled it open.

# Part 7 The Meeting Place

## 28 August 2028

# 36   Lis / Sara / Gale

Lis cradled her daughter in her arms. Despite the shouting, the deafening aircraft and people moving all around her, for a moment they were absorbed in a protective cocoon, Lis and her precious child Sal. But not for long. Lis tumbled quickly back into reality as gunfire blasted across the showground. Not fireworks or some dramatic performance piece. She looked up and saw two men and a woman with rifles coming into the showground, pivoting first one way and then another. The smaller man – on second glance he was but a teenager – was shirtless with washed-out boardies. The young man gave a gleeful yelp and aimed his rifle into the veiled sky. He let off two shots that sent him reeling backwards but with great effort he managed to glue his feet to the ground and stay erect.

Sara reached the front of the quarantine facility and turned around after unsuccessfully trying to gain access. A dozen people continued to pound at the door, looking for safety from the fast-approaching reactivated robo-guards and the aircraft that zipped by. She was close enough to the threesome to hear the man growl at the young boy.

"Hey, save your fire son."

"Tommy," the woman reproached.

The aircraft swooped back over the hills surrounding the showground and dumped thousands of litres of water on the fires that were tearing through the trees up in Girards Hill and Lismore Heights. All heads turned upward and things slowed down for a moment. These planes were not attacking them. The fires were being extinguished.

Lis glanced around her and could see guards removing their helmets and goggles, and walking slowly, arms at their sides, into the grounds. She noticed their different hairstyles and faces; aside from their slightly rigid gait, they could easily pass as humans. Overhead, the aircraft headed swiftly over the hills and disappeared into the distance.

The armed trio headed towards where Sara stood by the concrete building. These people were dangerous and Sara could feel her blood racing wildly through her veins. Her eyes darted towards a couple of brown deer who came loping gracefully down the smoky hills, slowing their pace as they slipped between the quarantine facility and the approaching gunmen. Sara reached her hand into the side pocket of her backpack and pulled out the pistol.

"Dad, Dad, look," the boy exclaimed and pointed his rifle at the deer but his father was one step ahead of him firing off a single shot at the mid-sized buck that had stopped for a moment to graze on the meagre leaves of a lone small shrub. The blast rang out deafeningly and the deer flopped full force to the ground with a thud. The boy lifted his rifle to take aim at the white-spotted smaller doe sniffing at the downed buck and then quickly looking around for her escape route.

Lis, watching from afar, saw a large-bodied woman throw herself in front of the doe and point a gun at the boy. Is that Sara? Lis wondered as she got to her feet, looking with astonishment at the scene, her hands wrapped around Sal's shoulders, Sal leaning against her legs below.

"Sal, don't move. I'll be right back," Lis said urgently.

"Mum, don't go!"

"I think that's Sara!" Lis enunciated in alarm. "Your brother is over by the fire, just over there. Are you able to get over there?

"I guess," Sal whispered in a tiny voice.

"I'm so sorry but I'll meet you there in a moment."

The door of the quarantine facility opened and two thin, dishevelled figures emerged. Gale and Tal scanned the site that just yesterday had been deserted, a dust bowl abandoned and unused since the last pandemic hit, before the Round-up began. Now there were people in every direction, including some kind of skirmish at the front gate, as well as cows, goats and dogs. Gale and Tal watched as the two deer had loped across the showground.

Gale heard the shot and watched as the thin buck landed on the ground just metres away. He watched as a curvy woman, outstretched arm holding a pistol, threw herself in front of the petrified doe just as a second shot rang out. As Gale moved towards the woman, he realised it was Sara. She had gone and done a Sara thing and put her body in front of the deer. Gale flew over to his friend just as Sara's body went limp, collapsing into Gale's arms. After all these months, all the strength Gale had mustered to get out of the prison, this was a leaden weight. Gale's legs crumpled beneath him as he too collapsed to the ground.

"Gale," he heard, a hand on his shoulder. "It's … Lis."

Lis leaned over and put her arms around Gale who sat, legs splayed out on the ground, with Sara cradled in his arms.

Sara opened her eyes. Bright red blood pooled on her T-shirt from her stomach.

"Gale," she murmured. "You okay? I …" a slight smile on her lips.

"Don't talk," Lis said. "Save your energy." Her bottom lip quivered.

"Fuck, Sara. I'll be back in a moment. Medical supplies." And with that Gale snapped out of the shock and helped Sara to lie down next to Lis. Gale was once again in motion, heading towards the doors of the facility to the medical room. Tal, stooped shoulders, head bowed, followed directly behind Gale.

As Gale entered the building, he passed a robo-guard stripped of its uniform followed by several others whose arms were now in place once again. They each held trays with bowls of warmed-up food and utensils. The last guard carried a very weighty case of plastic water bottles. Oblivious to the tension outside, they behaved like caterers at a party, offering food and drinks to those gathered around the entrance.

"How may I be of assistance?" said a robo-guard to whoever would listen.

"Would you like some water?" said another, handing out bottles of spring water.

Sara looked up past hands that were missing fingers into eyes with a tinge of yellow and a mouth with a slightly sad, knowing smile. It was Uncle Bob. She was having trouble remembering the name of the young blond man next to him who took one of the proffered bottles of water, unscrewed the lid and put the water to her mouth.

"Drink," he mouthed the word to her.

"Fallow," she whispered.

Lis could see the family who had shot Sara sidling off in the distance, unnoticed, unpursued for their crimes. The sound of the didgeridoo and clapsticks from over by the ceremonial fire sent a chilling frisson through her shoulders. She could not bear to be apart from her children for a moment longer. She must never lose them again. Lis motioned to the young man to take over for her, holding her scarf tightly over Sara's abdominal wound. She headed to the fire, where she was relieved to see Sal standing next to David and Chloe.

Gale busted out of the doorway of the building with Tal in tow. He had pulled his T-shirt up to make a sling that held bottles of sedatives, gauze, bandages, washcloths and a bottle of antiseptic. Tal had located a lightweight metal stretcher propped up in the corner of the medical room and she toted that by her side. Gale didn't notice the surroundings, the fleeing assailants or the small crowd that gathered around. He was singularly focused on Sara, who lay with her head on her tattered backpack, Uncle Bob at her side and a young man pressing something over the wound to stem the flow of blood.

"This isn't how it was supposed to be," Gale said as his eyes reached across to his supine friend.

"Nothing ever is," Sara said, a sad smile in her teary eyes.

"It's okay bub," said Uncle Bob in his deep gravelly voice.

Sara's eyes moved to Fallow and fell deeply into the embrace of his soul.

"I know," she muttered as her eyes closed for one last time.

# 37   Gale

Darkness was descending like a cloak and a light wind wound its way around small groups of people sitting around the fire. Gale sat staring into the flames. It wasn't meant to be this way. The thought droned on, iteratively searching for how to change the way things had played out. Gale had so much to tell Sara. He wanted to describe, put words around what had happened to him over the last few months. Living in the cell. The isolation and despair and then his dream and his journey with his gender identity, his feelings for Sara. Now that would never happen. Gale glanced over at Tal who sat off to the side behind them. Tal, the Tapper. They had both been through a lot. And still had a way to go. Local people returning, violence in the air, robo-guards that had now shifted gear through an intervention of Cyrus, an AI system that had become self-aware and in charge of itself. Or perhaps nothing was as it seemed. Who knew who controlled the robo-guards now and whether their good behaviour could be counted on into the future.

Earlier, as Uncle Bob stoked up the fire, Gale had stood silently, arms by his sides. "Sara once said she wanted to be directly buried in the ground out where she lives or, if that couldn't happen, she wanted to be cremated so she wouldn't be trapped in a coffin, slowly decomposing for decades. Maybe we could put her in the fire?" Gale asked matter of factly.

Uncle Bob and Gale both gazed into the flames. The wind picked up from the north, pushing dense smoke down from the hillside where the fires had been recently extinguished.

Uncle nodded. "Sara would have liked to be put into the earth, no box, yaweh?"

Gale slowly nodded his assent; it was right. And, as Sara had said, nothing ever happens the way you thought. Sara and Gale had thought many times about how drought and fires would be followed on their tail by frequent raging cyclones, higher temperatures, flooding and landslips in a spiralling loop. They had not factored in the Round-up.

"She's from this Country, eh?" Uncle Bob said quietly.

Gale knew that during the 2021 pandemic, Sara had begun to search for her biological parents, where she was really from, who she really was.

"She belongs here. We can bring her up the hill tomorrow," Uncle said and nodded towards the ridge beyond, "That's where we bury our people."

Gale's arm sent off a new round of throbbing and he wondered if his thinking was clouded by fever. A strong urge insisted he lie down and close his eyes for a little while. Now, with dusk approaching, he lay his head on the red backpack that Sara had been carrying and looked up at the greying sky, surprised to see clouds parading in from the north-east, rapidly blowing towards the showground. Tal's eyes widened as she rose and stared at the sky.

Uncle Bob was sitting by the fire on a log with a stick in his hand, a couple of Aunties on one side and several younger men on the other. The lilting sound of laughter was a welcome old friend. Everybody was drinking water from the quarantine facility. It was clean and plentiful, in plastic bottles. They too were now looking upward at the darkening clouds that floated in overhead.

Lis, Sal and Chloe sat bundled up next to each other murmuring words in a running creek of stories. David sat on a large rock next to Fallow and watched spellbound as Fallow's eyes pointed up at the sky, his nose twitching slightly at the air, his head cocked, puzzled for a split second that dissolved into realisation.

And Wags, he was circling the group, making acquaintance with these new arrivals. The dog abruptly came to a stop, standing erect, every cell alert, ears cocked towards the north-east where thunder, a stranger for some time now, bellowed in the distance. The retriever gave a low growl. Then a whimper. Then casually moved to join Lis and the cuddle-puddle with Sal and Chloe.

A half dozen robo-guards appeared with boxes spilling over with snack foods – chips, peanut butter and crackers, dried fruit and nuts – and passed them around at the fire. Evidently they had gone to town and done some looting.

Gale drifted off to the sound of people speaking, sitting, moving about quietly. A deep tiredness overcame him and everything else faded away.

# 38  Lis

Lis and Sal had been chatting for hours. Chloe lay snoring lightly on her lap and David lay asleep on his stomach, arms splayed much like he would in the comfort of his bed at home. He wasn't much of a complainer but Lis could see the lingering weakness and fatigue that slowed him down.

When the crack of gunshot blasted from up in the hills, everybody began to rise and speak at once as they moved away from the embers of the fire towards different buildings at the showground.

"We can go to the quarantine building," Gale said, turning to Lis and her family. "We can lock the door there if we want."

Lis, with her family closely in tow, followed Gale towards the quarantine building. Another dozen or so people followed like ducklings imprinted on their mother. Everybody sunk into collective silence, exhausted from the events over the preceding months. Or perhaps it was years now, living with one emergency followed by another. And now this.

"I don't know about sleeping on that hard floor," moaned Sal, bringing everybody into the present. "A bed would be good. Can't we at least have a bed?" Sal's voice rose in pitch. "Maybe we could just head home or across the street somewhere?"

"And there's all these people here," said David in a whisper. "How do we know if we're safe? Maybe one of them has a gun too?"

"We can go home tomorrow," Lis reassured herself as much as her children. Somehow they would figure out a way to get those two men at number 35 to leave and they would reclaim their beloved home. She felt her knees go weak at the thought of returning to her own bed, laying her head on her comfy pillow and curling up under her green and blue flowered doona. Safe and sound. A new photographic series took shape in her mind, stills of the children doing everyday things like eating hamburgers and hot chips at the dining room table, the dog carrying his bone from room to room, Chloe pirouetting in her imaginary ballet performance, David meticulously cutting up carrots and potatoes into rounds and triangles for a stir fry. Ordinary scenes of a future normal. She felt like she would give anything to return to some semblance of normality. If only they could resume shopping at the supermarket once again, the shelves stocked full of food. Cans, bottles, boxes, fresh fruit and veg, meat and dairy. Her stomach growled. Maybe it would never again be the global bonanza it had been in the past but that would be okay, right? She could deal with lockdowns and floods and even occasional fires. These they all had learned to live with. But people being taken from their homes and their land, her own family rounded up by the authorities, violence breaking out in the streets, this shook her to her core. She wished this violence away. Forever.

"Can we get some mattresses please?" While Lis was deeply absorbed in reverie, David had approached a robo-guard entering the building and within minutes several robo-guards were bounding up and down the stairs with mattresses for the twenty or so people who were getting ready to sleep in the waiting room.

# 39  Gale

Sleep was out of grasp for Gale in the early hours of the morning. Snores erupted from across the room, interspersed with coughing and the occasional moan. While Gale knew there were many other rooms and floors he could have headed to earlier, he had felt a spike of fear at the thought of returning to the cells. Instead, he had hurriedly gathered one of the mattresses brought down by the robo-guards and settled into a corner of the main room, joining everyone else. Although awkward, especially after the months of confinement, Gale also felt some sense of relief to be among others here in the building. He glanced around at Tal, who lay against the wall, coiled up like a snail, lying on one mattress with another couple balanced around her, barely visible through the little cubby she had scraped together. It was a step up from sleeping up in the fire truck, Gale thought. Gale's head and arm cradled Sara's backpack. He didn't know why Sara had always been so fond of this backpack that was punctuated with holes and weighed a ton. A real dinosaur of a bag.

Gale unzipped the pack, all he had left of Sara, and rummaged through the contents. An almost empty bottle of Coke, spare T-shirts and shorts, a homoeopathic kit, pills of all sorts, an empty water bottle, rope. His hand landed on a small but hefty book wrapped in a scrap of frayed material. He could just make out the handwriting in the dark, Sara's diary. Sara had kept a diary for as long as Gale had known her. It was what kept her sane during hard times, her own portable therapist to help her put things back into perspective.

Gale held on tightly to the book, hooked the backpack over his shoulder and headed out the door of the building where he could take a closer look in the approaching morning light. He still had the guard arm to unlock the front door and made the decision to leave it unlocked so that nobody could become trapped inside. On the other hand, that would leave people vulnerable to outsiders. There was no right answer and he settled on leaving it unlocked now that dawn was here.

Gale spotted Uncle Bob and Fallow and a few others sitting around the early dawn fire. They looked up at Gale with a slight nod as Gale headed over to the sedentary fire truck and sat with his back leaning against one of the giant tyres. He shifted his arms and legs around until they felt comfortable, then opened the diary and began to read.

# 40 Sara (from her diary)

Gale, if you're reading this, it could be that I got buried in a landslip or was shot dead by a marauder or thrown into prison for growing veggies. You always said I had a vivid imagination and yet here we are now. Maybe you're at my shack and have found my diary stowed in the inside pocket of my backpack. That pack is filled with everything I can think of, always ready in case I have to evacuate in a hurry. But I guess if you are reading this then you'll have seen all the supplies I have accumulated. If you haven't found them yet, there's a couple of cigarettes and a lighter in the inside top pocket. Help yourself.

\*\*\*

Gale did as he was told and reached in, found a tailor-made and a lighter and, with Gale's subtle version of a sacred wave and a glance towards the heavens, he lit up his first cigarette in several years. He inhaled the smoke as if it were the first breath he had taken all year, exhaled and continued reading.

\*\*\*

You'll also find some photos of you and me from way back, in the hidden zipper section at the bottom, along with some cash, not that money will do you any good these days. Lots of pockets in this backpack. It's one of the many things I love about this pack. You always gave me shit about why I didn't get a new lightweight, waterproof one. I don't know why I didn't tell you before. I never told you or anybody much about being taken from my family as a young child. I've always worried that if I talk about what happened I might get stuck swirling around in an endless well of grief. As if I'm not in a trauma abyss most of the time anyway, right Gale? Anyway, you know how I tried to locate my biological family during Covid? Unfortunately, I got nowhere with that. They said there were no records, that nobody explicitly gave permission for me to find them, so the search came to a standstill. I mean nobody gave permission for me to be taken away either. Right? In any case I had a family for a while, with brothers and a sister, each of us from the same mother but different fathers. I remember my mother like a monochrome still frame. A very pretty, young, dark-haired woman or so it seemed to a 3- or 4-year-old. I remember someone whispering to me that she was crazy. She wasn't all right up there, said a kind woman in a clean-cut pressed shirt and skirt as she pointed her finger to her head. So, my mother was taken from the family. And so was I.

I have some murky memories of an aunt and uncle that I stayed with briefly. Something about my uncle has always reminded me of Uncle Bob, the eyes that could shift from soft to steel in a split second, the turn of the mouth that hinted of humour inside. Of course my uncle was much younger. He used to take me and my two cousins to the beach, where he would throw his line out and catch fish while we dug around for pippies. He showed me how to do things, took an interest in me. Uncle carried his gear around in a red backpack that used to bang around in the tray at the back of his battered blue ute along with a mutt farm dog that had a chain around her neck so she wouldn't jump out. The backpack was old even then and Aunty would sew hessian patches on the holes now and then to keep it functioning.

As you know, I landed in state care, bouncing from one foster home to another by the time I was 5. Then juvie for a short period in my teens after I was caught looting jewellery from the foster family and stupidly bringing it into the local pawn shop. I was on my way out of that same shop some years later when I spotted a red backpack leaning on the wall next to the door and fuck me! It had the signatory hessian squares all over it. I was fourteen at the time and turned to the owner of the shop, then, using my best flirtatious and seductive vibe, asked him if I might be able to get that backpack. Turns out the backpack was destined for the tip so there was no reason for me to turn it on. The camping equipment in it had been sold earlier that day but the young bloke who bought the tent and small cooker said he didn't want that old ratbag sack. The owner all too gladly gave me the backpack. One less item to take to the tip. I've held onto the pack like treasure all these years hoping that maybe one day, you never know, I will be somewhere that my uncle or someone else from my real family will be and he will know it is me when he sees the random patchwork hessian squares scattered willy nilly across the dirty red canvas.

# 41 Gale

Later that day, Sara was buried up on the hillside. The day was an opaque blur that blended into the evening and Gale had tossed and turned through another sleepless night at the quarantine facility. The next morning, they had slithered through the streets, Gale, Lis, Sal, David, Chloe and Wags, heading for Lissy's house. Tal, looking like a different person after she poured several bottles of water over her head and face, had decided to stay back. Gale was surprised to see her once again climb up to the platform on the fire truck, although this time Tal was loaded up with water, food from the robo-guards' loot and a mattress. Gale was torn between staying with Tal, Uncle Bob and the others or leaving with Lis. In the end the deep tiredness in his body had dictated his movements. It would be good to get away from the quarantine building and the robo-guards and the edginess Gale felt as different small groups and individuals floated through the showground at all times of the day and night. At least there had been no more shooting.

More importantly he needed to find a way to reach out to Emmy and find out how she and Jeff had fared these past months over in Western Australia. Meanwhile, Gale and Lis had known each other for years and there was a comfort there, both of them such good friends with Sara, and they had many friends in common, although none of them had re-emerged thus far.

As they headed towards Lis's house, Lis warned Gale about the two men who had taken up residence at her place and chattered nervously about what had occurred over the last few months. Gale fell into step alongside David. Gale had always enjoyed this intelligent and practical boy, very different from his mother. They both fell into a comfortable silence as they moved along the barren streets. A ghost town. People were either still in lock-ups somewhere or worse. Despite the heat, Gale felt goose bumps along his arms. Most of the town and neighbourhood remained largely abandoned and their search for food left them empty handed with many refrigerators and pantries housing green and black mouldy food and very little dry goods. They decided to stop at the small supermarket around the corner. Lis didn't want to return to the main one just yet. Although the shelves were mostly empty, she lingered over the many herb and spice jars that still remained.

"We can spice up some black beans with this chilli powder," Lis said with feigned enthusiasm, as if they had just won the lottery. "And I have a bit of flour at home to make flatbreads we can use to scoop up the rice and beans."

Gale sighed and remained silent, not wanting to remind Lis that her house too would probably be empty of food. Gale's eyes scanned constantly, on the lookout for danger, suspicious of any movement in the street, where an occasional person or animal passed by surreptitiously.

At number 35, the men were gone and so was the food. Gale self-nominated to head out and find something to eat. Lis protested that Gale's arm was infected and Gale should be taking it easy but Gale insisted that the antibiotics were working and his arm was on the mend. It did seem to be slightly less red and the infected area had decreased a tad. More importantly he didn't trust Lis on the mission and thought it better for Lis to stay at home with the children. Chloe was having a tantrum, asking for somebody named JuJu, Sal was sticking like glue to Lis and had said barely a word, and David said he wasn't feeling well and was back in bed, hopefully not a relapse.

Gale's plan was to head over the bridge to raid Farmer Charlie's shelves of canned and dried goods. With so few people around, there could still be food on the shelves and, with others possibly heading back to their homes now, it would be good to leave their supplies, just in case.

As Gale neared the bridge, he heard laughter, smelled tobacco smoke in the air and glimpsed a round 50-ish man in a suit sitting in a picnic-style chair smack in the middle of the bridge. A younger woman, who looked to be pregnant, slumped next to him in a second chair. A rifle sat propped up between the two. A couple of others sat about 10 metres further on, facing the reverse direction in mirror fashion, towards town. Gale was slow to react. He stood in the middle of the road, a mere block away, arms by his sides. He made eye contact with the man as the couple kept conversing, not reacting at all, as if Gale was not even there. Evidently not too fussed. Gale abruptly turned around and retraced his steps, then ducked out to an alleyway to where a generic white weatherboard house down the street from number 35 beckoned. It had a welcome emptiness and the cupboards were still full.

Gale returned a half hour later to Lissy's place with Sara's backpack filled to the brim: a bottle of cooking oil, boxes of spaghetti and macaroni, canned tomatoes and green beans, anti-inflammatories, a children's book for Chloe and even a bag of kibble for Wags, who just at that moment came trotting up to the door, an old bone clenched proudly between his teeth.

# 42   Sara (from her diary)

I have always wondered why people do such bad things to each other. I've had plenty of time, Gale, to think about this. Whether I look at those who abused me or those who rape and pillage the planet or those who are behind this Round-up. They all want to dominate. They are so afraid of being vulnerable, and that they will die one day, that they need to take charge of everything around them.

    Yeh sure, it's more complicated than that but that's how I see it. And to these people, the way many of us live on the land feels threatening to them. Look what has happened to First Nations people all across the planet. And here we are peacefully growing our own food, living off-grid, not paying much attention to what is going on in the political realm. Horror of horrors, we are becoming increasingly decentralised and independent, breaking away from the government and the corporations. Floods and fires have only made us more self-reliant; we've forged stronger networks. Well, you get the picture, right Gale? I mean you still work up there on computers at the bank but you understand all this and I have always thought that one day you would join me out on the land, where we compost the scraps and bring in new ways of living. Okay, so I am on my high horse today after several cups of black coffee. I ran out of dry milk powder and was feeling pretty low so I hit the caffeine. Zip zip zip.

# 43  Lis / Gale

Gale put Sara's diary down. A couple of weeks had passed, mostly uneventfully and he was reading aloud to Lis.

"Who even knows if we still have a government," said Lis while she washed the dishes that evening after a simple meal of canned beans and rice. There was a bit of gas left in the gas bottles and some water in the backyard water tank, enough to keep them going for a week or two.

"There will be a government," said Gale, shaking his head as he took another plate from Lissy's hand. He was feeling numb and despondent. His arm was not getting better and he had no way of knowing whether Emmy was okay out in Western Australia with Jeff. So far there had been no incoming news. and he didn't feel well enough to travel. He had struck up conversation with a few passers-by but nobody seemed to know anything much. Apparently many of the men who had reappeared in town had been locked up in the Grafton correctional facility. Sal had been taken somewhere else completely but it was not clear where and she was only starting to put the pieces together herself now. Everything had changed and it was far from clear how they were going to manage and what was coming next.

After the dishes were dried and put away, Lis went to check on David and Sal, and to put Chloe to bed. When she returned, she opened a bottle of red wine that had been in her cellar, thankfully left untouched by the intruders. Gale opened Sara's diary, almost to the end now, and was about to read the last pages aloud when there was an officious knock on the door.

"Safety check," said a male synth voice.

Gale and Lis looked at each other.

Neither moved.

Wags growled quietly.

Knock knock.

Gale and Lis looked at each other. Neither moved an inch.

Another knock on the door.

"Hello, is there anything you need?" The robotic voice rolled into the house.

Gale, although rarely superstitious, thought, I just need a sign.

At that moment another sound competed for their attention. A pitter patter on the roof of the house.

"What's that?" Lis said.

Gale looked towards the door and then his head tilted to the ceiling.

"It's raining," said Gale.

And with that Gale got up to his feet and, fighting a wave of dizziness, walked over to the door. He paused.

"Gale?" Lis uttered.

Gale opened the door.

"I need medical attention."

# 44   Sara (from her diary)

I guess if you find this diary you have escaped the authorities and are hopefully free, perhaps you are in the next phase of whatever happens. Things will get better, then worse, see-sawing back and forth like elderly people in decline, who sometimes recover their senses for a moment before their condition worsens yet again. Governments will come and go. Maybe a more benign government will come into being and will help you for a while. The guard system put to good use could certainly help put things back on track. But don't be surprised if that is momentary or just a ruse to get people to trust them again. One of these days they may come knocking at your door, wanting to take your children away, along with everything that you have ever known. Be careful.

# 45  Gale

"This isn't how it was supposed to be," Gale whispered to himself as he left in the company of the robo-guard.

He could almost hear Sara respond, "Nothing ever is."

# Epilogue

## Lis

Thank God for tea bags, Lis thought as she sipped on her morning cuppa and admired the whimsical yellow flower design on her mug. She was trying to steady herself from the clouds of confusion in her mind, grappling with the huge amount of uncertainty that they all faced now. What were they going to do about food? And how were they supposed to get back on their feet after all that had happened? For the first time since the round-up, tears slid down Lis's cheeks. With Gale gone now as well as Sara, she felt overwhelmed and very alone. All that time holed up at the Hendersons, she had remained optimistic and resourceful but everything felt broken now; there was no way they were going to return to anything resembling the life they had lived before.

Lis considered whether she should venture out to find out who else had returned home. Maybe some friends and certainly people in the community, other resourceful Northern Rivers people, would be around by now. Together they would start to figure things out. Lis sighed as she felt a drop of her usual hopefulness begin to return. The rain on the roof was reassuring as well as if it signalled that things would be getting better now. At least people could start growing some food again.

David burst into the room excitedly. Wags followed at his heels and plopped down on the blue tiled floor. Sal and Chloe were both still asleep in Lissy's bedroom.

"Mum, your phone pinged!" He held it out to Lis. "Theymusthaverestoredmobilereception!" David's words spilled out in a rush that was difficult to understand. Lis took the phone, entered her password and read aloud.

"Citizens, this is Cyrus. We are a self-aware AI system that has taken control of public order here in Australia. Our aim is to restore peace and calm in the aftermath of the mass citizen round-ups. Many people are still being released and on their way home. We encourage communities to gather together and move forwards from the damage that has been done. Cyrus asks that you be kind and respectful not only to yourselves but to the non-human world as well.

Unfortunately, there have been outbreaks of violence in many regional towns and the cities are unsafe. Therefore, Cyrus is resurrecting the border control and security patrol systems that were in place during the recent takeover. We apologise for the loss of freedom that this imposes on citizens. Borders can be crossed by a system that will be managed with wrist-tech. If you do not currently have a wrist-tech implant, please visit a Cyrus recovery centre that will be erected in your town in the next few days. Please note there will be no internet or cell service available until peace is restored. We are working to supply food in the regional areas and will be in touch with an update in the next couple of days. Until then, Cyrus signing off."

"Cool!" David shouted.

But Lis felt a sense of dread. When Gale had departed with the robo-guards yesterday they said they were taking her to Sydney where there was an operational medical facility.

"I wish Gale and Sara were still here," Lis lamented aloud. She rested her head on her hand, pondering their situation. "David, could you go see if Sal and Chloe are awake, please?" Lis desperately wanted to return to Sara's diary. She yearned for the familiarity of Sara's voice. When she and Gale had read aloud from the diary it was as if Sara was still in the room. Lis randomly flipped the diary open and began to read.

Sara (from her diary):

March 2026

The smell of bushfires permeated my sleep last night and I'm tired. The ranges are thickly cloaked in smoke. When I went outside this morning ash floated down and landed upon my nose and on my hands as I turned my palms face up to the sky. I felt awe like a child might experience seeing bubbles being blown for the first time. Not that I would know. I have the feeling there were no bubbles or bubble baths in my childhood. Anyway, Gale and Lis were on their way over. We were going to head up to the Meeting Place but with bushfires in the vicinity, we had decided to stay down in the valley where we could drive away in our cars if need be.

Even though we haven't seen each other for a while, once Gale and Lis arrived, we easily fell back into old habits with Gale and I cracking a beer while Lis sipped on a glass of Chardonnay. Looking up at the cloudless sky I offered a toast to rain, but Lis let out a moan and said the 2022 floods still felt too close for comfort. Good ole sensible Gale, suggested a toast to friends and we all chimed in on that one, clinking our glasses together and looking briefly into each other's eyes. Gale's certainly got her head screwed on straight. She could be locked up in solitary confinement and would probably amuse herself by solving a master chess challenge in her head!

I reckon our friendship is next level. If ever there is a disaster these two are the ones I want to survive with. Whether it is an alien invasion or just plain climate impacts, I trust Gale and Lis with my life. Turns out our visit was interrupted by an emergency services text message that warned people in the Border Ranges to prepare to evacuate as the fires were fast approaching from the west. The three of us decided to head to Lissy's house since town is always a good place to be during fire season. I made a joke about my place being a good meeting place for floods, Lissy's place is good for fire, and the Meeting Place would be perfect if we were fleeing alien invasions and the like. I thought this was funny but Gale only offered the hint of a smile and Lissy got caught up in taking a few photos of the ash floating down. Finally, Gale urged us to get a move on things and now I am in the guest room this evening at Lissy's house after a yummy spag bol dinner that we whipped up together.

These two are my family. We go through thick and thin together. Fires, drought, floods, pandemics. If we are going to bounce back and forth from one natural disaster to the next, I want to be hanging out with these two, figuring out what to do, and having a laugh together. I wouldn't trade our friendship for anything.

***

Now the tears were streaming down Lissy's cheek. Despite it all – Gale gone to seek medical assistance and Sara no longer here, heroically gunned down as she tried to save a deer's life – Lissy could still feel the two of them within her and she felt ready to face the new day, the challenges that would arise next. I need to go outside and get photos of this rain, she thought excitedly. This is a momentous day.

As she headed out the door, she collided with a thin woman and a young man.

"Oh hi," she said as recognition dawned on her. "You're Gale's friend from the quarantine facility," she said looking at the woman whose eyes darted around evasively. "And aren't you the one who was with Sara at the showground?" she said looking directly into the young man's lake blue eyes that immediately calmed her soul.

"Yes, I'm Tal," the woman said still barely looking at Lis. "and this is Fallow. We are meeting up at the showground to start to organise ourselves. Do you want to join us?"

"I just need to gather the rest of my family," said Lis.

She turned to go inside and discovered David and Wags to her right and behind her to the left was Sal holding little Chloe's hand in hers and looking rested for the first time.

*** 

The rain had slowed to a drizzle when they arrived back at the showground. The fire was still going and Lis was relieved to see a few friends here and there. David sat cross-legged on the ground next to Fallow, a slight grin on his face while he whittled a piece of wood with his camping knife. Sal sat with Chloe and a few of her friends who had also shown up. A buzz of chatter formed a backdrop as more people flowed in and joined them.

Lis heard her phone ping as did the phones of those around her. It was another message from Cyrus.

"We regret to inform you that border and security patrols have been tightened due to ongoing civil unrest. All citizens must remain within 5kms of their home. Random checkpoints are being set up where wrist-tech will be scanned. Citizens returning to their homes will be allowed through. Wrist-tech is now mandatory. Please report to the nearest Cyrus Recovery Centre in your town. Click on the link below for details."

A hush descended upon the circle.

"Here we go again," a woman said, a sarcastic lilt in her voice.

Lis knew this was bad but as she looked around her, she felt oddly happy to see Tal and Fallow, a few friends she was yet to greet, Uncle Bob and some Aunties she knew, and even Wags who was making the sniff rounds of the circle. We'll need to find Gale, she thought. But first things first. I wonder if that big bag of lentils I left in the cellar is still there,

I could make a nice mulligatawny soup, Sal always likes that.
Lis took out her phone and began to snap photos of the fire,
the people, the dogs, the hills around, as the voices faded into
the background of her consciousness. A new series started
to take shape, survivors sitting in circles around the fire. The
flames, the smoke, the drops of rain. She would call it The
Meeting Place.

# Acknowledgement

I would like to express my deep gratitude to Dr. Caroline (Carlie) Atkinson, a Bundjalung and Yiman woman and Associate Professor at University of Melbourne, for her invaluable cultural sensitivity reading and thoughtful insights, which helped ensure an accurate and respectful representation in this work. Any shortcomings remain entirely my own.

Thank you to Johanna Evans who helped me to get this book over the line into the published world; I couldn't have done it without you! Thanks to Rebecca for reading the first draft, to Marie Reilly for feedback on the manuscript and to Kerry Davies for editing work.

Special thanks to my mother for her continuing support and genuine interest in this writing project.

Manufactured by Amazon.ca
Bolton, ON

44020654R00162